Apollo reached out and wrapped his fingers around Elle's wrist, holding her hands still. "What the hell are you doing?" he asked, his voice a growl.

She looked up at him, her green eyes round, those soft, sassy pink lips shaped into a perfect O. "I…" Color flooded her face.

"If you were thinking you were going to take my shirt off, either stop now and walk out that door, or keep going and realize that I will have you flat on your back and screaming my name in a *very* different way before you can protest."

Her color deepened…her eyes grew even wider. He thought she would run. Because Elle was a *good* girl. And she was stone-cold, aloof, and fancied herself far above him.

It had made him want to destroy that façade from the first. He hadn't. Because he knew that she was innocent. Knew that she was nothing more than a cosseted rich girl who would be completely out of her depth with a man like him. A man who had grown up on the streets in Athens—who had learned the hard truths about life early on. About loss. About the true nature of people.

He had known that if he ever touched her it would violate the trust he had built with her father.

But if she was going to touch *him* now, if she was going to remove the barrier that had always loomed between them, then he wasn't going to put a stop to it.

THE GREEK'S NINE-MONTH REDEMPTION

BY
MAISEY YATES

First Published in Great Britain 2016
By Mills & Boon, an imprint of HarperCollins*Publishers*
1 London Bridge Street, London, SE1 9GF

© 2016 Maisey Yates

ISBN: 978-0-263-06461-2

Our policy is to use papers that are natural, renewable and recyclable
products and made from wood grown in sustainable forests. The logging
and manufacturing processes conform to the legal environmental
regulations of the country of origin.

Printed and bound in Great Britain
by CPI Antony Rowe, Chippenham, Wiltshire

Maisey Yates is a *USA TODAY* bestselling author of more than thirty romance novels. She has a coffee habit she has no interest in kicking, and a slight Pinterest addiction. She lives with her husband and children in the Pacific Northwest. When Maisey isn't writing she can be found singing in the grocery store, shopping for shoes online and probably not doing dishes. Check out her website: maiseyyates.com.

Books by Maisey Yates

Mills & Boon Modern Romance

Bound to the Warrior King
His Diamond of Convenience
To Defy a Sheikh
One Night to Risk it All
Forged in the Desert Heat
His Ring Is Not Enough
The Couple who Fooled the World
A Game of Vows

Princes of Petras

The Queen's New Year Secret
A Christmas Vow of Seduction

The Chatsfield

Sheikh's Desert Duty

One Night With Consequences

Married for Amari's Heir

The Call of Duty

A Royal World Apart
At His Majesty's Request
Pretender to the Throne

Visit the Author Profile page at millsandboon.co.uk for more titles.

To Jackie, Megan and Nicole for listening to me say,
'This is weird. I'm not doing it right.
I don't think this is good enough!'
every time I work on a book, and helping me through it.
Every time.

CHAPTER ONE

SOMETIMES ELLE ST. JAMES imagined taking a pen and stabbing it straight through Apollo Savas's chest. Not to kill him of course. He didn't have a heart so the wound would hardly be fatal. Just to hurt him.

Still, other times she fantasized about crossing the boardroom, wrenching free the knot on his tie and tearing the front of his shirt open, scraping her fingernails down his heated skin and feeling all those hard muscles beneath her hands. Finally. After nine long years of resisting him, resisting the heat that roared through her body every time their eyes met.

That one was *way* more disturbing than the stabbing thing.

It was also far too frequent.

They were sitting in a crowded meeting and she should be paying attention. But all she could think about was what she would do to him if she had five minutes with him, alone, behind a locked door.

It would either be violent or naked.

He was talking about budgets and cuts. And she hated those words. It would mean scaling down her team again. As had been the story of the past twelve months, ever since he'd bought her out from her father's holding company. A company that had since sunk into bankruptcy.

Just another moment in a long line of Apollo undermining her. Finally, her father had been forced to give her responsibility. Since his stepson had finally proven to be a viper in the nest, so to speak.

She'd been installed as CEO. Then Apollo had come down like a hammer.

It was his fault. At least in part. And nothing would convince her otherwise.

She had a plan. A plan he seemed intent on thwarting at every turn. She knew she could rescue Matte without all of these sweeping staff changes, but he wouldn't give her a chance.

Because—just as he'd always done—he was making it his mission to undermine her. To prove he was better even now.

But that didn't stop her eyes from following his hands as he gestured broadly, from wondering what those hands might feel like on her skin.

She could write what she knew about sex on a napkin. The sad thing was, it would be two words.

Apollo Savas.

He'd been sex to her from the moment she'd understood what the word *sex* meant. From the moment she'd understood why men and women were different, and why it was such a wonderful thing.

The dark-haired, dark-eyed son of the woman her father had married when Elle was fourteen. He had been fascinating. So different from her. Rough around the edges, a product of his upbringing in a class of society Elle herself had had no contact with. His mother had been a maid prior to her marriage to Elle's father. The culture shock had been intense. And very, very interesting.

Of course, since then he'd grown into a dark-hearted

man who'd betrayed her family and put her under his boot heel.

Still, she wanted him.

The Big Bad Wolf of the business world, huffing and puffing and blowing your dreams down.

"Don't you agree, Ms. St. James?"

She looked up, her eyes locking with Apollo's, her heart thudding a dull rhythm. The last thing she needed was to admit she'd missed what he was saying. She would rather admit to having fantasies of killing him than the alternative.

"You'll have to repeat the question, Mr. Savas. My attention span for repetition isn't infinite. This is the same song you've been singing for months, and it isn't any more effective or logical than it was last time."

He stood, his movements liquid silk. She could see from the black glitter in his eyes that she was going to pay for her words. The thought sent a shiver down her spine. Fear mingled with unaccountable lust.

"I am sorry you find me boring. I shall endeavour to make myself more interesting. You see, I was speaking of the fact that for a company to be successful it must be sleek. Well oiled. Each cog functioning at top capacity. Extraneous cogs are unnecessary. Sluggish cogs are unnecessary. I was attempting to be delicate with my metaphor." He began to walk down the length of the boardroom table, the postures of each person he moved behind straightening as he did. "Perhaps I would have held your attention a bit better if I would have simply said that if I identify a portion of your company functioning at less than optimum capacity I will start slashing and burning your employees like they were dry brush."

Her entire face felt like it was on fire, her heart pounding harder now. She clenched her shaking hands into fists. "Everyone in this company—"

"I'm sure your speech is about to be inspiring and truly emotional, but since this is not a feel-good under-dog sports movie, you should perhaps save your breath, Ms. St. James. You can say what you will, but I have seen the numbers. Conviction doesn't equal profits. I will be reviewing everything closely and making cuts at my discretion. With that, I think the meeting is adjourned. Ms. St. James has a very low tolerance for my droning, I hear. If it is the same for the rest of you, you should be pleased to be sent on your way."

The collective surge of bodies making their way out of the room reminded Elle of a herd of wildebeests fleeing a lion.

A big, bored lion who wanted nothing more than to scare them by flashing his teeth. He wasn't going to give chase. Not now.

No, now his focus had turned to her.

"You are in rare form today, Elle."

"I am in exactly the appropriate form, *Apollo*," she said, reverting to the use of his first name.

They were *family*, after all.

Not that she'd ever seen him as a brother. A sexual fantasy she didn't want. Her biggest competitor. Her darkest enemy. He was all of those things, but not a brother.

"I own your company," he said. "I own *you*." Oh, dammit all, why did those words make her...ache? "You never seem to show me the proper amount of fear."

"Real leaders don't rule with an iron fist," she hissed. "They understand that intimidation isn't the way to gain respect."

She shouldn't be talking back to him, but she could never control her tongue around him. They'd known each other for too long. Had spent too many years in the same household.

And she had spent too many years tearing strips off him when she'd felt like she had the upper hand. When she was the blood daughter of her father, the one who held a rightful place in their upstate mansion.

Things changed. Oh, how things changed.

"Says the woman who is no longer in a true position of leadership." He smiled. Showing his teeth.

She wouldn't scatter. She would not. She was not a wildebeest.

"Oh, but I am. As long as Matte is an independently operating entity beneath your large corporate umbrella, I am here to run it as best as I can. I am here to stand in the gap for my employees and give you the information black-and-white printouts can't."

"You're being ridiculous. Everything is electronic now. I'm not wasting resources on printouts."

He turned and started to walk out of the office. "You know what I mean. A flat, two-dimensional report reducing everything to statistics and cold numbers is hardly the be-all and end-all."

"That's where you're wrong," he said, taking long strides down the hall.

Elle had to take two steps to his one, her high heels clicking loudly on the marble floor as she hurried after him. "I am not wrong. It doesn't offer the whole picture. You can't possibly know how the company is really functioning. How each worker impacts the creative process. Matte isn't just a magazine. It's a line of cosmetics, a fashion brand. We have books and—"

"Yes," he said, stepping into an elevator, "thank you, I am very familiar with how my assets function."

"Then you should be aware of the fact that I have strategies in place that require all of the manpower I possess. Initiatives that take time to launch but will catapult this brand into worldwide recognition."

"Yes. So you said last time we met. And, unlike you, I don't drift off in meetings."

She growled and charged into the elevator after him. "I did not drift off."

He pushed the button to the lobby and the doors slid closed. Then he turned that dark, unsettling focus onto her. The air around them seemed to shrink, rendering the already crowded space impossibly tight. "No. I don't believe you did, Elle," he said, his voice as silken as his movements. "You were looking at me with a great deal of intensity. Too much to be on another planet entirely. What was it you were thinking about exactly?"

"Driving a pen through your chest," she said, smiling.

Because she would be damned if she'd say, *Tearing your clothes off and seeing if you're as good in reality as you are in my dreams.*

Even though she felt like that reality was written all over her face, across her skin in the red stain of a blush.

He offered her a wry smile. "You know I can't be killed like that. You have to cut my head off and bury it in a separate location to my body."

"I'll let the hit men know." She turned and smiled at him again, and he offered one in return.

The doors slid open, revealing the rather vacant bottom floor. Matte shared its offices with many other businesses, and with penthouses on the top floor. At this hour of the day not many people were coming and going.

"Where is it you're staying, Apollo?" she asked. "A crypt somewhere in Midtown?"

"The one just next to yours, Elle," he said, his tone light. "After you."

He extended his hand, waiting for her to step out of the elevator. She swept past him, moving through the lobby and going through the revolving doors. She stepped on to the busy Manhattan sidewalk, put her sunglasses on and stood there, tapping her foot.

Apollo emerged a moment later, straightening his suit jacket and standing across from her for a moment.

"Care to continue shouting at me while I walk?" he asked.

"I'm not shouting at you. I'm calmly explaining to you why you're wrong in your methods of handling my company."

He turned away from her, walking down the crowded street, his broad back filling her vision.

"Apollo!" Okay, she was shouting now. "We are not through with our meeting."

"I think we adjourned it."

"The general meeting," she said, upping her pace. "But *we* are not done."

"I'm just here," he said, gesturing to an old boutique hotel only two buildings down from the Matte offices. "Since I'm in town primarily to deal with Matte I thought I should stay close."

"Congratulations. How sensible."

"I have my moments. Judging by the fact that I'm a billionaire who successfully staged a takeover of your father's company, I've had several moments, actually."

"If you were as clever as you think you are you would listen to my plans for Matte. The answer isn't to reduce us down to nothing. You have to let me try and expand it, otherwise we really will die."

"You're assuming I'm trying to save you, dear Elle. Perhaps I just want to pull the plug."

"You… You…" She was sputtering now. She never sputtered. She blamed him.

"Villain. Scoundrel. I answer to any of those really."

"You have always been a competitive son of a bitch, but this is above and beyond."

"You're assuming this is a competition."

"What else could it be? You're ungrateful. For everything my father gave you. And for the fact that he didn't give you everything."

He chuckled, a dark, humorless sound. "Oh, you mean that he didn't give me his corporation, or Matte, in the first place? Why do you think he installed you, Elle? Your competence? No. He gave you the position to keep a foothold once I bought him out."

The words landed hard, hollowing out her midsection. Leaving nothing but a crater behind.

Like you didn't suspect that already.

She had. Of course she had. But the fact he knew it meant it was obvious. Possibly to everyone.

The doorman opened the golden door for them and Apollo paused to tip him before continuing on. Elle opened her purse and produced her own dollar, handing it to the man before going in after Apollo.

She was not allowing him to do her tipping for her.

"I am in the penthouse suite. It's very nice."

"Why am I not surprised that I just got out of a meeting where you were discussing tightening belts for my company, and yet you're staying in the penthouse suite."

He pushed the button for the elevator and the doors slid open. She followed in after, starting to feel slightly out of breath.

"I am not in need of money, *agape*, if that's why you thought I was mentioning cuts."

Agape. She hated that. He'd started using that on her

sometime when she was in high school. Just to make her angry. And some small part of her grabbed hold of it every time, holding it near. *Love.*

Oh, what a ridiculous, stupid...

She really hated her hormones.

"Why else would you mention cuts?" she asked, keeping her tone sweet.

The doors slid shut and she had the uncomfortable feeling of being trapped in a closed-in space again.

"Because *you* need the money. Matte needs the money. In a digital world your print publication is lagging and while you have certainly come up with innovative ways to compete, you haven't leveled out yet."

"But if you have enough—"

He chuckled. "I don't run a charity. I run a business. My corporation turns profits. That's what it does. I make money hand over fist, and I'm comfortable admitting that. I'm proud of it. But that won't continue if I don't refine my assets. Refining is a hot and painful process. It takes fire. And people being fired."

"Ha-ha. You're far too funny for your own good."

He frowned. "Was that funny? It wasn't meant to be."

The elevator stopped and the doors opened on a narrow hallway. Apollo stepped out and walked down a few doors, pausing to open it. "Come in," he said.

She very much had the feeling of being a small, vulnerable creature invited into the lair of a predator.

You are not a wildebeest. You are just as scary as he is. You are a lioness.

She stepped over the threshold and into the room. It was lovely, he was right. Ornate moldings and trim framing the space, the windows looking out over Central Park.

There was a large seating area with a bar, and off to

the left an open door that she could see led to a bedroom with a very large, dramatic bed.

She imagined, as tall as he was, he took up most of the mattress. That thought made her picture him—long, tanned limbs sprawled out on the bed. Would he look more relaxed in sleep? Would he seem less…lethal out of that custom-fit black suit that conformed to every line, every muscle in his body?

He closed the door behind her with a finality that made her jump.

"My team is the best there is," she said. "They have some of the most creative minds in this—or any—industry. You have to admit the fact that the Matte Guidebooks have been hugely successful. And the makeup guide actually helped to increase sales of the cosmetics. It was specific to the brand and that—"

"Again you are telling me things I already know. I didn't get to this position in life without paying attention. I understand that your team is important to you. But if I don't do what must be done, if I don't make the hard cuts, none of you will have a job."

"But I—"

"You seem to be under the impression that this is a democracy, Elle. Be assured, absolutely, that this is a dictatorship. I am not negotiating with you. And it is only by my good graces that your pretty ass remains in the CEO's office."

Heat and fury washed over Elle in a fiery baptism. "And here I thought it was because I'm good at my job."

"You are," he said, taking a step toward her. "But there are a great many people who would be good at your job. People who didn't get handed their position from their daddy."

"Oh, that's hilarious, Apollo. As if you didn't get a leg

up from my father, you Judas." She took a step toward him, rage propelling her now. "My father treated you like one of his own children. He put you through school."

"And I excelled on my own."

"Then you stabbed him in the back."

"I bought him out for much more than thirty pieces of silver, little girl. Perhaps what really hurts is the fact that you were betrayed by your father, not by me. He put you in this position knowing you would fail."

She gritted her teeth, doing her best to shake off his words. To not allow them to take hold. All of this reached down deep. To old wounds. To the way she'd felt she couldn't measure up to Apollo, the son her father had always wanted. To her own fears of being eternally inadequate. And he knew it.

She would not let him win so easily. "He trusted you. When you offered to help he didn't imagine you dismantling everything."

Apollo lifted one broad shoulder. "He made a mistake in trusting me."

"Clearly. You would betray not only the man who set you on the path to success, but your own mother."

"She's fine. Your father is hardly financially ruined. She continues to enjoy her status as his wife. And again, Elle, need I remind you your father sold Matte, and some of his other holdings, to me of his own free will."

"You had him in a position where he couldn't say no."

Apollo took another step toward her. He was so close now that she could see his eyes weren't completely black. She could see a faint ring of gold that faded to copper, then to deep brown. Could see the dark stubble beginning to grow in at his jawline.

Could smell the scent of his aftershave and skin.

"Interesting you put it like that. If dire financial straits take away choice you could argue my mother had little choice in marrying your father in the first place."

"That's ridiculous," Elle said. "She wanted to."

"Did she?"

"Of course."

"A cleaning lady offered the chance to live in luxury after years barely making it in the US? After years of homeless poverty in Greece?"

"That isn't... It has nothing to do with this."

"Maybe," he said. "Or maybe the point is that you can always say no, Elle." He leaned in. "Always."

She could barely breathe, her head swimming, her entire body on high alert. She was almost certain she had no blood in her veins, not anymore. It was molten lava now, heating her from her core.

She remembered so clearly feeling this way every time he brushed past her in the halls of the family estate. Every time she caught sight of him at the pool—his lean, muscular body so fascinating to the girl she'd been.

Only once had they ever come so close to each other. Only one other time had she ever thought he might feel the same forbidden desire that she'd felt from the moment she'd set eyes on him.

Apollo is going to be your new stepbrother.

Everything in her had rebelled at that, immediately. Because she had seen him and wanted him in a way she knew would be wrong once their parents were married. So she had distanced him. She had been...well, sometimes she'd been terrible. But it had been for her own survival.

It was even worse now. He was still her stepbrother. But now, any affection she'd ever felt for him had been twisted by his betrayal. She should have stopped obsessing about him a long time ago.

But she hadn't. She couldn't. She was a slave to this, to him. Always.

She hated it. She hated *him*.

And she had spent nine years resisting him. Embracing the anger, the annoyance and everything else she could possibly use as a barrier between her desire for him and her actions.

Giving in would be a failure. In terms of her self-control. In terms of her relationship with her father. What would he think if he knew she wanted Apollo? What sort of scandal would erupt if the media knew she was helplessly attracted to her stepbrother?

So she had denied it. Pushed it down deep. But she had been aware of it every time she saw him. Every glance. Every accidental brush of his hand against hers. Every time she went to bed at night, hot and aching for something she knew only he could give her.

But he had bought out her father's company. He was gunning for Matte. Her father had installed her as CEO to keep some connection to the company—just as Apollo had said. And she'd failed spectacularly.

She could feel everything slipping out of her grasp. The company. Her control. Everything.

And she'd never tasted him. Never had him. This man who was destroying her whole life. Who commanded her fantasies and called out the deepest, darkest desire from deep inside of her.

For what? For appearances. To triumph.

There would be no triumph here. She was losing. Utterly. Epically.

Why not have this? Why not have him?

It was all going to burn to the ground. She might as well go up in flames with it.

She could see his pulse throbbing at the base of his

throat. If only she had a pen in her hand. It would be so easy from this position to stab him clean through with it. But she didn't.

So instead, she reached up and grabbed hold of the knot in his tie, and wrenched it free.

CHAPTER TWO

APOLLO SAVAS DIDN'T entertain daydreams. He was a man of practicality and action. When he wanted something, he didn't sit around fantasizing about it, he took it.

That was the only reason he knew that it was no hallucination that Elle St. James, his stepsister and mortal enemy, was currently stripping his clothes off, her eyes bright, glittering with rage and desire.

He had resisted her, this, for years. Resisted her. Out of deference to the man he considered a father. Out of respect for all he'd been given.

But all of it had proven to be false, had proven to be a lie. And still he had roped Elle off. Had kept her separate—in many ways—from his plans for revenge.

And David St. James had known he would. Because whether she knew it or not, he had always protected Elle. She had always mattered.

But things had changed. And now she was tugging at his tie. And he was tired of restraint.

He reached out and wrapped his fingers around her wrist, holding her hands still. "What the hell are you doing?" he asked, his voice a growl.

She looked up at him, her green eyes round, those soft, sassy pink lips shaped into a perfect O. "I…" Color flooded her face.

"If you were thinking you were going to take my shirt off, either stop now and walk out that door, or keep going and understand that I will have you flat on your back and screaming my name in a very *different* way before you can protest."

Her color deepened, her eyes growing even wider. He thought she would run. Because Elle was a *good* girl, by the standards of her father. Though, she was stone-cold, aloof and fancied herself far above him.

It had made him want to destroy that facade from the first. He hadn't. Because he knew that she was innocent. Knew that she was nothing more than a cosseted rich girl who would be completely out of her depth with a man like him. A man who had grown up on the streets in Athens, who had learned the hard truths about life early on. About loss. About the true nature of people.

He had known that if he ever touched her it would violate the trust he had built with her father.

But if she was going to touch him now, if she was going to remove that barrier that had always loomed between them, then he wasn't going to put a stop to it.

Apollo Savas was a man who took what he wanted.

With one exception.

Elle.

He had wanted her from the moment she'd transformed from a girl to a woman. A haughty, rude woman who walked by him with her nose in the air half the time. Perversely, it had always made him want to have her even more.

She thought his hands were dirty. Thought he was beneath her. It made him want to put his filthy hands all over her. Made him want to pull her right down with him.

His biggest betrayal had never been buying St. James

Corp's most valuable assets and breaking them off piece by piece.

No, his biggest betrayal had started long before he'd discovered David St. James's true nature. It had begun long before he'd discovered the dark secrets surrounding just why he and his mother had been brought into the St. James home.

His first betrayal had been in the way he'd looked at Elle.

But everything was shot to hell now anyway. Every allegiance broken with his "family." Why not this, too? Why not slaughter the last sacred cow?

He had destroyed everything else. He might as well destroy this, too. And he would relish it.

Her hand was still frozen, holding on to his tie. Then, her eyes took on a determined glitter, her lips curling into a snarl as she yanked hard on the silken fabric, pulling it free from its knot.

He growled, grabbing ahold of that sleek high pony-tail that had been taunting him from the moment he had walked into the boardroom today. He wrapped his fingers around her coppery hair and pulled hard, tilting her head backward. Her nostrils flared slightly, her lips parting.

They held their positions for a moment, staring at each other, clearly waiting to see what the next move was.

He had waited too long. He was not waiting another moment.

He would have her now. Strip away every prim and proper layer. Punish her with his kiss as he should have done that day she'd dared him at the pool. The only time the anger between them had given way and revealed the layer beneath.

Of course, she had acted as though nothing had happened after. And so had he.

But he would make sure this time she would not be able to act unscathed after he was through with her.

He wrapped his arm around her slender waist, drawing her up against his body as he backed them both toward the wall. It stopped their progress ruthlessly, her shoulder blades pressed firmly against the hard surface. He bent his head, kissing her neck, his teeth scraping her skin.

The sound that escaped her lips was raw and desperate, her hands clutching his shoulders, her fingernails digging into his skin through the fabric of his suit jacket. Then she slid her palms down flat, grabbing hold of the front of his shirt and tugging hard, sending buttons flying as she wrenched it open. She pushed his jacket from his shoulders, grabbing hold of his shirt and shoving it down, too. He unbuttoned the cuffs, helping her and her progress, and untucking it from his pants and throwing it down onto the floor.

She looked completely shocked, and wholly satisfied by her actions as she regarded his body. Then she pressed her palms to his chest and slid her fingers down to his stomach, her fingernails scraping him lightly as she did. She grabbed hold of his belt, making quick work of that, as well.

"Greedy," he said, taking hold of her wrists and drawing her arms up over her head, holding her there with one hand as he set to work on the buttons of her silk blouse with the other.

She fought against him, the color in her cheeks deepening, her breasts rising and falling with the shallow gasps of her breath. He chuckled when her shirt fell open, revealing an insubstantial red lace bra and he imagined she thought it made her seem daring.

She arched her back, thrusting her breasts into greater prominence. He tightened his hold on her, pressing her hands more firmly against the wall. "You don't get to set the terms," he said. "Not in the boardroom, not in the bedroom. I am in charge in *all* things."

"Always a competition with you, isn't it?" she asked.

"Oh, *agape*, it has never been a competition. How can it be when I always win?"

For the first time, he saw a slight flicker of doubt in her eyes. But it was quickly replaced by a challenge. "So insecure that you have to exert your dominance in such a cliché fashion? You are exactly the same here as you are in the office."

He leaned in, his lips a whisper away from hers. "You're going to pay for that."

"I hope this isn't an empty threat, Apollo," she said, the words throaty, enticing. "You seem to be full of those."

He closed the distance between them, closing his teeth around her bottom lip and biting her. She gasped and he pulled away. The flush in her cheeks had spread to her neck, had down to the full swell of her breasts. She might be angry, but she was aroused, too.

"One thing you need to learn, *agape*, is that my threats are never empty. It's simply that the consequences might be delayed in coming."

She looked down, then back up. "I do hope the coming isn't terribly delayed today."

Those words, coming from Elle's lips, seemed shocking. From any other woman it might have been commonplace dirty talk. Not even all that dirty when it came down to it. But from Elle? It had the desired effect.

He was so hard he thought he was going to burst through the zipper on his pants. His heart was raging, his hand shaking as he undid the last button on her blouse and pulled it from her shoulders.

He couldn't remember the last time a woman had affected him in such a way. If one ever had. But then, he had never been in a situation quite like this. His partner had never looked at him with lust and rage burning from her eyes all at the same time. She'd never looked quite like she wanted to strangle him and have her way with him in the same moment.

And, he had never been with Elle.

"I didn't realize you were a dirty talker, Elle." He scraped the edge of her ear with his teeth. "If you had been negotiating this way all along you might have been a lot more successful."

"You're a bastard," she bit out, turning her head and tracing the line of his jaw with the edge of her tongue. "A complete and utter—"

"And you want me," he said, releasing his hold on her and drawing his face back, pressing the tip of his nose against hers and meeting her fierce gaze. "So what does that say about you?"

"Oh, I know that all of this is the final nail in the coffin of my decency." She grabbed the end of his belt buckle and yanked it through the loops, then set about working on the closure of his slacks.

"Go out with style, I say." He slid his hands down her slender waist, to the full curve of her hip, and down farther, gripping the hem of her skirt and shoving it up roughly over her hips. No surprise, her panties were the same red lace as the bra.

Not that he was complaining.

"I took you for a white cotton kind of girl," he said. "Who knew that you had so many secrets?"

"You're never going to know my secrets, Apollo," she said.

"So venomous," he said, his lips touching hers now as he spoke the words. "And yet, you're dying to have me."

She put her hand between them, pressing her palm against his hardened arousal. "Same goes."

"I'm tired of talking."

And then, he crushed his mouth to hers, claiming the kiss he should have taken years ago.

Elle had no idea what she was thinking. She wasn't thinking. She was feeling. Feeling everything. Rage, need, arousal like she had never known existed.

She would like to be confused about this. About how this could happen. About how she could be doing this with a man she hated so very much. But lust and anger had always been twisted up together where Apollo was concerned. Well, maybe not always. But in the past few years. And that was when her desire for him had turned from a girlish crush into a woman's need.

She wasn't sixteen anymore. She knew what men and women did in the dark. She didn't need her own hands-on experience to be aware.

But somewhere, during all of that, Apollo had gone from being someone she trusted and admired—a member of the St. James family—to their bitterest enemy. And somewhere, as that change had taken place, her desire for him had changed, as well.

And now it was this strange, twisted thing that she couldn't begin to untangle. And there was no other man who made her feel anything near what he made her feel.

It didn't matter that it was sick. It didn't matter that it was wrong. What Apollo made her feel was pure adrenaline. Pure excitement. Even if it wasn't all good.

He made every other man she had ever gone out with seem like a bland, beige substitute.

That was why this was happening. Really, it was why it *needed* to happen. When this was over, she would finally be cleansed.

Her need for him would go down in one fiery ball of pleasure and rage. And when she looked at him she would feel...nothing.

Oh, she wanted that more than anything.

She kissed him back with all of that. All of the anger, all of the lust. His tongue swept against hers, his hold on her hips firm, blunt fingertips digging into her skin. Then he shifted his position, putting his hands between her thighs, stroking his fingers over the thin lace that concealed her desire for him.

She gasped, everything inside of her shaking. She had never been this intimate with a man before, and yet she wasn't afraid. She wasn't experiencing any virginal nerves. She was more than ready for this. It was the combination of years of fantasies. An explosion of... Well, of everything.

His fingers slipped beneath the fabric, gliding through her slick flesh. If he'd had any doubt about how much she wanted him, he couldn't doubt it now.

"Yes," he said, the word a growl.

The way he said that, the absolute, incontrovertible evidence of how much he wanted her in return radiated through her. Spurred her on. She grabbed hold of the waistband of his pants and underwear, tugging them down his lean hips. There was no place for tenderness here, no place for hesitation.

She reached between their bodies, wrapping her hand around his hardened length. It was her turn to shudder, her turn to growl. She had never touched a man like this. She had no idea he would be so very big. She was nearly weak with wanting him. This was why she felt hollow. This was what she needed to be filled.

He slipped one finger inside of her and her breath hissed through her teeth, the unfamiliar invasion shocking and immensely pleasurable.

She took hold of his arms, clinging onto his rock hard biceps as he continued to tease her with a preview of what she really wanted.

She looked up at him, her heart hammering in her chest. He was beautiful. There was no question. And she wanted him. She wanted him more than she'd ever wanted anything in her entire life. It was important that she know it was him. As if it could be anyone else. As if anyone else could ever make her feel this way. This exhilarating mixture of destructive anger and impossible need.

She kissed the corner of his mouth, tracing his lower lip with the tip of her tongue. He moved his hand from between her thighs, lifting it, grabbed hold of her bra and pulled it down, revealing her breasts to his gaze. He lowered his head, drawing one tightened nipple deep into his mouth.

Sensation shot through her like an arrow, hitting her low and deep. A low, harsh sound escaped her lips and she let her head fall back as she laced her fingers through his hair, tugging hard as he continued to pleasure her.

"Please," she whimpered, "please."

He moved away from her, then bent down grabbing ahold of his pants, pulling his wallet out of the pocket before producing a condom.

Her breath gathered up in her chest like a ball and held there, a heavy weight she couldn't move. She could only watch him. Look her fill at his beautiful, masculine form. He was even more beautiful than she had imagined.

He returned to her, his bare chest pressing against

hers as he flattened her against the wall. She looked at his face, his gorgeous, thoroughly despised, utterly beloved face.

She grabbed hold of him, bracketing his face with her hands and tugging him forward, kissing him hard and deep. He put his hand back between her thighs, this time pushing two fingers into her, stretching her gently. She was so ready for him. Beyond ready.

"Do it," she said against his lips.

He moved his hand, gripping hold of her hips, sliding one hand down her thigh and lifting her leg, opening her to him. He tested her slick entrance with the blunt head of his arousal. Then he thrust deep inside.

The pain was sharp, swift. Tears stung her eyes, and she shut them quickly because she didn't want him to see. She didn't want him to know. She had felt powerful a few moments ago, but this made her feel a lot more vulnerable. Vulnerable was not what she wanted. She wanted pleasure, she wanted her desire satisfied. She wanted to rid herself of this toxic, intense feeling she had for him once and for all.

But, she hadn't anticipated this. Not just the pain, but the feeling that she was breaking apart. The feeling that they were connected, closer than she had ever been with anyone.

Somehow, she had imagined the fact that she hated him might buffer against any other emotions.

But it didn't.

So she kept her eyes closed.

If Apollo noticed, he didn't comment. Instead, he fused his mouth to hers and flexed his hips, a flash of pleasure slowly overtaking the pain.

Slowly, all the discomfort began to recede. And she just wanted him. There was nothing else. There was no ugly history between them, there was no anger, no hatred. Nothing but an intense, burning need to be satisfied. She clung to him, to his shoulders, her lips pressed to his as he established a steady rhythm, pushing them both toward the brink.

He thrust hard and she let out a hoarse cry, raking her nails down his back. He growled, his rhythm faltering. And then, there was no more steadiness. There was nothing but a frantic race to the finish, his movements rough, intense. And she took it all. Every last bit.

He gripped her chin, tilting her face up, forcing her to meet his gaze. And she did. She didn't look away, unwilling to flinch in the face of his challenge. She shivered, tension growing more and more intense in the pit of her stomach, her internal muscles gripping him tight as her orgasm began to build.

He slowed his movement suddenly, withdrawing slowly before pushing back in hard. White light broke out behind her eyes, release exploding inside her like a bomb, a wild burst of aftershocks radiating through her, leaving her shaken, weak. And then he followed, his entire body going stiff as he shuddered out his own release.

He lowered his head, his teeth digging into her collarbone. She let her head fall back against the wall, a sigh escaping her lips.

They stood like that, for just a moment. And then slowly, reality started to creep in.

She had done it. She had given her virginity to Apollo Savas.

And suddenly, horrifically, all she wanted to do was curl into a ball and cry.

She pushed at his shoulders, and he withdrew. She began to look around at the ground, realizing that only her shirt had been entirely discarded. Everything else was simply askew. That was—frankly—slightly more embarrassing than the alternative. She hadn't even waited for him to undress her completely.

He would think she was completely desperate. He would think that she had been yearning after him for years.

It was the truth. Which was what made it particularly horrifying.

She straightened her clothes, tucking her skirt back into place, fixing her bra as she pulled her blouse back on. He said nothing. He simply watched her with those dark, unreadable eyes.

She smoothed her hand over her hair.

"Too little too late, *agape*," he said.

She froze, her hand still poised over her undoubtedly wrecked ponytail. "Excellent," she said, her voice so brittle she thought it might break.

"I am leaving in the morning."

"All right," she said, the words hollow, echoing in her head.

"I will not see you. I will not make any decisions about staffing changes until the next time we meet."

"I'm relieved to hear that."

"I'll be back in town on the twentieth. Make sure you keep your calendar clear."

With that, she could see she was dismissed. With no more fanfare than if they had simply finished a meeting.

And he was still naked. It was absurd. But she wasn't going to highlight the absurdity. Not when she simply wanted to get out of there as quickly as possible so she could have a complete and total meltdown.

"Then I'll see you on the twentieth."

She collected her purse, drawing the strap over her

shoulder and clinging tightly to it. To keep herself from…
Slapping him? Kissing him again? She wasn't certain.

"Excellent. Should I call you a cab?"

"No," she said, checking her watch. "It's… It's only three o'clock. I have to go back to work."

She had to go back to work like this. With the impression of his hands still on her skin, her cheeks burning from the brush of his whiskers against them.

"So it is."

"Goodbye," she said.

He tilted his head. "Goodbye, Elle."

CHAPTER THREE

ANTICIPATING THE TWENTIETH had become something of a
reverse Christmas countdown. In that she hoped it would
never come. It might have been nice to have an Apollo
Advent calendar though. So that every time she thought
about him arriving she could eat a piece of chocolate to
try to deal with her stress.

When she arrived at the office that morning it was
with an industrial-strength coffee, a bottle of ibuprofen
and a very fake smile plastered to her lips.

Because Apollo was due to arrive—who knew when—
to start handing down edicts from his high horse. And
she was going to have to face him for the first time since
they had… Since that day in his hotel room.

The very thought of that made humiliating color wash
through her face. That day had been an aberration. Something that would never be repeated. She had, after all,
gone the first twenty-six years of her life without sex.
She should be able to happily get through another few
weeks. Then, maybe when everything settled down, when
Apollo stopped coming in and poking at her employees,
reshuffling her business and in general upending her
life, she would contend with the fact that she needed to
find a relationship.

That was the problem. She had simply waited too long.

She had allowed Apollo and her desire for him to become so large in her mind that nothing else could compare.

Well, now she'd had sex. With Apollo, as it happened. So, question answered, tension diffused.

She was a modern woman. She wasn't going to allow him to make her feel ashamed about her actions. Even though, considering he was a relic of a man, he would attempt to make her feel ashamed. If for no other reason than he would be actively attempting to assert his dominance over her.

Well, no thank you. She was…indomitable.

She gritted her teeth, opening the door to her office and nearly dropping the coffee in her hand when she saw who was already sitting at *her* desk. "That's my seat," she said, the words coming out crisp and harsh.

"It's lovely to see you too, *agape*."

"Now, Apollo," she said, deciding that she was going to be the one to address the elephant in the room before he got a chance. It was there, she might as well be the one to name it. "Don't try to sweet-talk me just because we had sex."

"I wouldn't dream of it," he said, his lips tipping up into a smile.

"No, I suppose you wouldn't. That would require you to know how to sweet-talk."

"You rocked my world. I saw God. You have ruined me for all other women."

She gritted her teeth against the strange, ridiculous warmth that flooded her when he spoke. He was being a jerk, and she knew it. So his words shouldn't make her… anything. She took a fortifying breath.

"What you said," she said, waving her hand. "Sub-stitute 'men' for 'women', 'slightly disorganized' for 'rocked', and 'God' for... I don't know, maybe 'a really good cheesecake'? Not exactly divine, but adequate."

"You are in *typical* form today."

"I try for consistency, Apollo. It's part of my charm."

"I have rarely seen evidence of your charm. Your *charms* perhaps, but I'm not really speaking of your personality."

"Right, well, for some reason things have been especially difficult between us lately, haven't they? Though, I imagine not as difficult as things have been between you and my father. Have you spoken to him since you rammed that knife into his back?"

"Oh, yes. Of course we have."

"You're sick. How could you do that to your own—"

"He is not my own anything. I am not your blood, *agape*. And a good thing to or what happened between us would be off-limits. Both in the past and in the future."

She gritted her teeth, trying not to blush. She was definitely playing at being slightly more blasé and experienced than she was. But he hadn't called her on it yet. So she was going to carry on. "I would rather run my new Jimmy Choos through the shredder, thanks."

"Is that what the kids are calling it these days? I admit, that doesn't sound very sexy."

"It wasn't meant to be."

"Right. Tell me, Elle, how is my mother?" he asked.

Elle arched a brow. "How long has it been since you've spoken to Mariam?"

He shrugged. "Months? She doesn't approve of my betrayal any more than you or your father do."

"And yet you don't feel any guilt over it?"

"I have my reasons," he said, his tone so cold and hard it could cut glass.

"I'm sure you do, but none of them are compelling

enough for me or my family. I don't care what your reasons are. And your mother is well," she said. "I just talked to her last night."

It had been difficult to talk to her stepmother when memories of what had passed between her and Apollo had lingered so persistently. She had felt...guilty and completely transparent. Thankfully, Mariam had her own topics to discuss and hadn't seemed to notice Elle's general silence.

"Well," she said, clearing her throat, "as charming as this little detour has been, let's get down to business."

He reached up, touching the knot on his tie. "Oh, you meant *actual* business."

"You're a pig."

"I'm wounded. Now, I've been going over projections for the quarter. You have to either increase profits soon or you need to start cutting expenses. I can guarantee one, but I can't guarantee the other." He stood, placing his hands on the desk. *Her* desk.

She tried to cling to her anger. Anger that would hopefully be much more powerful than the attraction that was still surging through her. What was her problem? She was supposed to be cured. She was supposed to have inoculated herself to all future Apollo encounters. Cure yourself from a snakebite with snake venom, and all that. But she didn't feel cured. She did not feel at all inoculated. In fact, she felt a little bit dizzy.

"Of course you can't," she said, the words coming out harsh. "No one can guarantee a profit increase. But trust me, if we keep on going in this new direction—"

"This isn't about trust. It's about the bottom line. I have a great deal more experience in business than you do, Elle."

Those words rankled. In part because they were true.

In part because they dug beneath the suit of armor she had worked so hard to put into place today. It hit the wound beneath it that twinged every day. That she was her father's second choice through and through. When she failed at this, she would prove that she never should have been here in the first place. That if her father had had his way he would have put someone else in her position. That if Apollo weren't too important for it, if Apollo hadn't turned against them, it would likely have been him.

You decided failure be damned, remember?

Yes. She had. But it was difficult to feel committed to that now.

"But I care about this company."

"As do I. It's a part of my bottom line, and there is nothing I care about more than my bottom line."

"Well, Matte is only part of your bottom line because you set out to acquire it when you saw that it was floundering. You knew what you were getting."

"And without my influence this company would probably already be six feet under. Like the rest of the holdings I bought from your father."

"You fired the final shot into them."

"A mercy killing," he said, his tone hard. "Don't oppose me, Elle. I am not doing this for my own amusement. If I succeed, you will succeed along with me. I am not the enemy that you set me up to be."

She didn't know what to say to that. Except, it was a disagreement they were not going to settle. Not without blood anyway. "Yes, but you said you were standing there ready to pull the plug, so let's be honest. You aren't a savior, either."

"I never claimed to be."

"Well, don't stand there and pretend that you aren't the villain."

"Oh, did you think that's what I was doing? You're wrong there. I know full well that I'm the villain here, *agape*. If I had a mustache I would twirl it. Alas. You will have to settle for the assurance that I know full well where I stand in this little play. However, we do not have to oppose each other. I know that my presence is sinister. However, there is nothing you can do to fight it. But understand I will save Matte if it's at all possible."

"You're here to announce cuts today, aren't you?"

"Surprisingly, no. But I did come to discuss something with you."

"What?" she asked, feeling suspicious.

"I would like for you to come to my European headquarters. To get a little bit of an idea for how things run, to attend to some meetings there, and to attend a certain number of charity events."

"What?"

"What I would like to do is help revitalize the image of Matte. I would like to bring you into the public eye. Have you as the public face, so to speak. With a little bit of help you could provide a facelift all on your own. And then, maybe we would be able to avoid cuts."

She hadn't expected this. She was, in fact, struck dumb by the fact that he was extending a hand out. That he was offering her a chance to not only save the company, but to do it in such a public way.

She had been prepared to be the one left standing in the ashes. A phoenix who was not poised to rise. She had been prepared to go down in flames, with her hands on Apollo's naked body.

And now…now he was changing things. Again.

"You just expect me to pick up and go to Europe with you?"

"Yes. And I don't exactly expect you to have a major issue with being asked to spend some time in Greece with me."

"Your headquarters are in Greece still? Are you the last remaining corporation in the country?"

"I am successful. Worldwide. It would be a poor thanks to my homeland to remove the jobs and revenue I provide simply because there's been some unrest."

"Please, don't tell me you have a heart. Only a moment ago you were telling me that your decisions were based on the bottom line."

"I *don't* have a heart. I simply have a strong liking for dolmas and ouzo."

"That I can believe."

He smiled, and for a moment, she felt like she was looking back at the boy he had been. The boy she had known all those years ago. The one who had captivated her from the first moment she had laid eyes on him.

The boy she had proceeded to snipe at and torture with flippant remarks every chance she got. Reminding him that he wasn't really a St. James. Because she'd been nothing more than a little girl with a crush and she'd handled it like they were on the playground.

But though things had never been easy between Apollo and her, he'd been very close with her father. But as close as Apollo and her father had once been, they were just as distant now.

And she had been thrown into the middle of that divide. Tossed into a storm she could never hope to weather. Between two alpha males locking horns. One defending his turf, the other intent on destroying it.

So take control. Do this.

"Well, I'm not going to complain about a free vacation," she said, trying to keep her tone light. She wasn't going to show her hand. Not to him. Wasn't going to let him see that this mattered to her. That she was going to use this—whatever it was to him—to gain a handle on things again.

To redeem herself.

"Oh, this isn't going to be a vacation," he said, rounding the desk and making his way toward the door. "We will go to Greece and work. Additionally, there is a charity event in Athens that we will attend together."

"As business associates," she said, "I assume."

She couldn't even imagine her father's reaction. If he had any idea that she and Apollo— He would be furious. Disgusted.

The idea of disappointing him like that...of losing him altogether, was something she couldn't fathom.

Her mother had left when she'd been a child. She could barely remember her. But she remembered the hole left behind, because it was still there.

She couldn't go through that again.

Apollo gave her a dismissive glance. "What else would we be? The entire idea is to strengthen the brand. Should there be any suspicion that the two of us had—"

"There's no need to keep bringing it up."

"You're the one who seems to persist in bringing it up."

Elle crossed her arms, shaking her head, her ponytail swinging back and forth. His eyes followed the motion.

"You should wear your hair down," he said.

She abruptly stopped shaking her head. "I didn't ask you for fashion advice."

"And yet, I'm giving it. Because you desperately need it." He looked at her, his expression critical. "Yes, you need a slightly younger look. One that isn't quite so... ironed."

"Well, my clothes are ironed. Would you have them look rumpled?"

"I would have you look slightly less like a matron."

She frowned. "I do not look matronly. I have a very classic sense of style. It's chic."

"You certainly know how to flatter your figure." He didn't bother to hide that he was looking. "But you need more than that to be the kind of brand that people remember."

"I'm not a...brand," she sputtered, "I'm a woman. Where are you going?" He had walked past her, heading for the door.

"I thought I might go and speak to some of the staff."

"No," she said, hurrying after him. "I do not wish to unleash you on them. I don't want you talking about how their jobs may be in jeopardy when you make final decisions."

"Their jobs may well not be in jeopardy if you don't fight me every step of the way. People like a public face. You can provide that. You can be strongly associated with the brand, and in effect, become a brand yourself. A young, professional woman. Brilliant, fashionable. You can be that woman."

She rolled her eyes. "That does not sound like—"

"It isn't a negotiation. Either you comply with my plan, or you are subject to Plan B, which is making sweeping cuts and doing my best to lift profit margins that way."

She made an exasperated sound, following him down the hall. "I wish you wouldn't keep walking away from me."

"I have places to be. I want to take a look at the different departments. Get a body count. So to speak."

"We are *talking*." She scampered after him. "Of course I will agree to go."

He pushed the button for the elevator. "I'm glad to hear that. I get the feeling sometimes you're just opposing me for the sake of it."

"And I get the feeling that you're an ass to me just because you enjoy it."

He chuckled and she stepped in just as the doors began to close. "Well, you are possibly correct in that assessment. Anyway, you spent a great many years being an ass to me simply because *you* enjoyed it."

She let out a harsh breath and watched the numbers on the elevator as it moved. Suddenly, she was very aware of the fact that she and Apollo were alone again. She looked at him, just a quick glance out of the corner of her eye. She tried to ignore the restless feeling between her thighs. Tried to ignore the restless feeling in her body.

After what seemed like an eternity, the doors opened again, and they were on the floor that housed the marketing department. He stepped out of the elevator and began to sweep his way through the space like a destructive wind. As he whipped by, heads turned, expressions went from relaxed to terrified.

"See that? Your mere presence lowers morale. I hope you're happy."

"I don't care about morale." He paused by one of the desks. "Hello," he said, clearly attempting to be charming. "My name is Apollo Savas. I'm the owner of this company. What is it you do?"

The girl, a blonde who could barely be twenty-five, blinked rather owlishly. She seemed to be struck dumb by his presence. Either by the fact that he was the owner of the company, or by the fact that he was just so damn good-looking. Truly, it was a problem. Elle felt a moment of sympathy for her.

"I'm on the marketing team for the makeup line," she said, looking a little bit thunderstruck.

"Have you been satisfied with the performance of those products?"

"Well," she said, shuffling the papers on her desk around, "we have seen an increase in revenue this past quarter. And our relationships with vendors—"

"How do you plan to continue the increase? What do you think attracts consumers to this product? Why should they buy this instead of say…any other brand of lipstick? I am a man, I know, but I'm not certain why one sort of cosmetic might be more attractive than another."

"I… I…"

"Enough," Elle said. "You do not need to prod at my staff."

He turned toward her, an amused expression on his face, and suddenly she felt like they were the only two people in the room. That little blonde might as well have evaporated into thin air.

There was no question, she was not remotely as immune to Apollo and she would like to be.

Apollo would question the purity of his motives if his motives were—in fact—ever pure. They weren't, so he was certain there was something self-serving and wretched behind them now. Even if he didn't know precisely what.

He had wanted to impress upon Elle the importance of her complying with his plan. When he had left her after… After the appalling lack of control that had occurred in his hotel room, he had formulated a plan to try to improve things for her company. A foolish thing, perhaps. He didn't know why he should care about the fate of her magazine. Beyond the fact that it was a potential profit machine for him.

Perhaps it was the fact that she had become collateral damage in a war he'd never intended to bring her into. But David had placed her in direct line of the firing squad.

Apollo wasn't a kind man. At least, no one ever accused him of being so. And he had never made it a goal to be seen that way. He had cared about very few people growing up, and it had turned out those he had cared about most had betrayed him long ago.

And so he had stolen his stepfather's empire, started dismantling it. But he had left Elle at Matte. God knew why. He'd known in the end he would destroy it, destroy her.

Perhaps it was because he knew what it was to be caught in the consequences of the sins of the father. Hers and his. Perhaps because he knew that—whether or not Elle had been kind to him when they were younger—she was innocent here.

But now...now it was as though a veil had been stripped away from his eyes. He would have to use her. There was no other choice. There was no preserving her. That much had been made clear when he'd taken her against the wall.

It had been symbolic in many ways of that protection being destroyed. That desire to keep her safe from himself being completely and utterly ripped away.

He could no longer ignore Elle. Could no longer dance around the fact that he would have to destroy her along with her father.

He would use her. And he would discard her.

It had nothing to do with his desire to strip her naked again. To watch her pale skin flush with pleasure once more. It had nothing at all to do with that, because he was not going to allow himself the indulgence.

Indulgence was unacceptable. But revenge? That was sweet.

"Perhaps you would like to give me a tour of the rest of the department, Elle?" he asked, ruthlessly cutting off his train of thought.

"Of course."

They moved away from where they had been standing, and she continued on down the role of desks. "Just don't *talk* to anyone," she said, her voice hushed.

"Why is it that you think you can tell me what to do when I am in my own company?"

"Because I am the boss," she said, her tone sounding slightly petulant. "That has to count for something *somewhere*."

"Sadly for you, I am your boss. Being boss of a lot of other people doesn't give you extra clout. I am the final word. So let it be written, et cetera."

She swept through the little space quickly. "There you have it. And now, I expect you want to be going."

"No," he said, crossing his arms across his chest. "I'll head back up to your office floor and set up for a few hours, get a few things done. I do like to familiarize myself with my acquisitions."

Elle looked livid. Her jaw set, her lips in a flat line. "Can't you do that in your hotel room?"

The mention of his hotel room brought back illicit memories. "I could. But I want to get a greater sense for how things are running here. It is in your best interest to keep me around. I might grow attached. I might yet see the importance of this team you keep talking about."

She said nothing, but her expression took on a rather long-suffering edge. They walked back through the office space and toward the elevators again. She pushed the button, then pushed it again when the elevator didn't immediately appear.

"If I didn't know better I would say you were in a hurry to escape my presence."

"I *am*," she said, flashing a smile. One he very much wanted to kiss right off her pretty face. But he was still calculating. When. Where. What. He wouldn't touch her until he made those decisions.

If he touched her at all.

"I do admire your honesty," he said, instead of kissing her.

"What is taking so long?" She scowled, hitting the button again. Then suddenly, the doors slid open.

"Tenth time's the charm," he said, stepping inside.

She gave him a withering glance before moving inside after him.

The doors slid shut and he had the impression that all the air had been sucked out of the space.

The tension between them was unlike anything he had ever known before. Likely because she was the only woman he had ever bothered to resist. He could remember well the first time he had noticed her as a woman, rather than a girl. Sometime after her seventeenth birthday, when all of her snubs and cutting comments had begun to arouse even as they enraged.

When they'd given way to fantasies of him showing her how base and beneath her he truly was.

His attraction, swift, sudden and abhorrent to him, had hit him low and fast in the gut, so quickly he had not had the chance to guard against it. He had not expected to have to guard against an attraction to his chilly younger stepsister.

He had nearly acted on it back then.

He could well remember the time he'd come home from university to see her getting out of the pool. Sleek curves barely concealed by a hot pink bikini that should have clashed terribly with her red hair, but rather was all the more enticing for how incongruous it was.

And he'd gone over to her, and she'd said something snotty, as she usually did. Then he'd grabbed hold of her arm, and pulled her to him. Her green eyes had gone wide, those pink lips parting gently. Begging to be kissed.

But he hadn't. He'd watched the water drops roll over her bare skin, over her breasts, had imagined lowering his head and slicking up the slow-rolling water. But he hadn't done that, either.

He'd waited. Waited until her eyes had darkened with desire. Until he'd seen her breath speed up, the pulse in her neck beating at a rapid rate. He had held her arm until he'd been sure he'd turned her on. Until he'd been sure the little ice princess was hot all over.

Then he'd let her go, and turned away, hard as iron and fantasizing about what he might have had.

And now... Well, now he'd had her, hadn't he? He had answered the question he'd never meant to ask.

He looked at her now, at the sleek ponytail that begged for him to grab hold of it, to wrap it around his hand. Her long, elegant neck. The soft curve of her pale lips. His stomach tightened. Clearly, his lust for her was not so easily dealt with via one quick screw up against the wall.

"I wish you wouldn't do that," she said, pressing the button that would take them to the floor that housed her office.

"Do what?"

"I wish you wouldn't stare at me."

"I'm trying to unlock the mysteries of your mind," he said. "Or rather, I'm attempting to remember what you look like underneath your clothes." He knew that taunting her was the wrong decision. Knew that it would only push them back to the place he was so desperate to stay away from.

You don't want to stay away. You want her naked and panting in your arms again.

"Stop it," she said.

"You're so desperate to forget what happened between us."

"Nobody likes to remember rock bottom, Apollo. I consider having sex with you my own personal walk through the valley of the shadow of death."

"I'm honored, I'm sure."

"Honored isn't what you're supposed to be." She arched one finely groomed brow, her lips twisted into a sneer. She was so self-righteous when she was just as guilty as he was. So sure she was above this attraction that burned between them when she was just as enslaved.

He wanted her. The angrier he got with her, the more he wanted her. Whatever this thing was, the sick, twisted desire that was exploding between them, he couldn't measure it or assign a number to account for it. He couldn't parse it the way he could a business acquisition. It wasn't the simple desire he felt for the sort of woman he usually picked up to spend a few hours of fun with. It was much, much darker.

It was forbidden. Something he had told himself he couldn't have.

Perhaps that was why it was coming to bite him in the ass now. He didn't typically practice restraint. Maybe by creating forbidden fruit, by placing it in the middle of his personal garden and telling himself he could not eat it, neither could he touch it, he had created temptation.

That made the most sense. Since Elle looked like original sin. A brilliant, shining apple he wanted to bite into.

And why shouldn't he? His reasoning for resisting her didn't matter now. He didn't want to honor her father. And he still wanted to kiss that puckered expression off her face. So why the hell not?

"You don't like me," he said, that darkness compelling him now. "And yet, you do want me."

"Come now, Apollo, don't tell me you like every single one of your bed partners. We both know that sex isn't love," she said, tilting her chin upward, a faint blush spreading across her cheekbones, adding a kind of dissonance to her bold words.

Elle was certainly playing the part of experienced woman. She had gone up in flames in his arms, an equal participant in the conflagration. And yet, it didn't all ring true. Didn't quite piece together in a way that made sense.

He wasn't sure he cared to analyze it. It wouldn't change his actions either way.

"Perhaps. But sex and hate don't typically go together," he said. "And you claim to hate me."

"I do," she said, green eyes flashing. "I hate you for what you've done to my father. To me."

"Not enough to leave the company."

"That would be abandoning it altogether. What he built. What he's trying to keep hold of, in spite of you. I won't do that."

"I do admire your dedication. Your loyalty."

"Why do you admire my loyalty? You don't possess any of your own."

"We admire the things in others we struggle with ourselves, do we not?" he asked.

"I wouldn't know. I certainly don't admire anything in you."

He chuckled, turning to face her, closing some of the distance between them. Her eyes widened and she backed against the wall. It reminded him a little bit too much of what had happened the last time they had been alone in an enclosed space together.

"I think there are a few things you admire about me," he said, moving in a little bit closer. Her eyes widened, her pupils expanding, the green in her eyes reduced to a thin ring. Her mouth dropped open, soft and round, and begging to be kissed. To be explored. "You most certainly admire what I can do to your body. I think we both know that."

"I *do* possess some restraint," she said, her voice trembling.

"Do you?" he asked, his voice sounding rough, ragged even to his own ears. "Perhaps we should test it."

He reached out and hit the stop button on the elevator, his stomach tightening, feeling as though a fist had closed around it.

He reached out and took hold of her arm, mimicking that day out by the pool.

"You want me," he said. "Admit it."

"I will not," she said, reaching out, shoving him. But then her hand lingered on his chest, her breasts rising and falling with her rapid breathing. She looked up at him, her eyes wide, terrified.

"You want me even now," he said.

And it felt imperative he make her admit it.

She tapped against his chest with her fingertips before slowly curling her fingers around the material of his shirt.

Then she pulled him to her, kissing his lips hard, deep.

He tasted anger, and a hint of shame on her tongue. And he knew just how the two mixed together, because he felt it, too.

She groaned, pushing away from him suddenly, but he wrapped his arm around the back of her head, holding her steady, working his fingers through her thick, red hair. "You want me," he growled, "don't deny it."

"Wanting isn't the same as having."

With his other hand, he opened the top button on her blouse. "It's the same for us."

"It doesn't have to be," she said, sounding desperate.

"I think it does," he said, his voice rough. He didn't know himself. Not at all.

She reached between them, pressing her palm over his hard length, stroking gently through the fabric of his dress pants.

"I dreamed about you," she said, her voice hushed, her words rushed. "About this."

"So did I," he said, placing his hand over hers and increasing the pressure of her touch. "Every night."

"Have you had another woman since you had me?" she asked, her tone fierce.

"No." He suddenly thought of her touching some other man like this. "Have you had another man?"

She shook her head, curling her fingers around his arousal. "No."

He growled, pulling her into his arms and kissing her, rage and relief burning through him. The very idea of another man putting his hands on Elle made him angry. He wanted her. It had been too long. Nine years. Nine long years lusting after Elle St. James, even as he hated her family. Even when he was overtaken by the desire to see their destruction, he wanted her. It was unacceptable.

He would burn it out. He would burn it out and then it would be over. Afterward, he could discard her if he wished, but this would finally end.

He stripped her clothes from her body as quickly as

possible, nearly tearing the delicate fabric of her blouse in his haste. Definitely tearing her panties.

She didn't protest. Instead, she made a sweet little sound of pleasure as he wrenched the lace fabric away from her skin, as he stroked his fingers over her wet flesh, so slick, so perfect. She wanted him. There was no denying it, no faking it.

He could feel the evidence for himself.

He stripped all of her clothes from her body this time, leaving her completely bare to his gaze. He had spent so many years fantasizing about what she might look like. The size of her breasts, the color of her nipples. That beautiful thatch of curls at the apex of her thighs.

Yes, he had woken up from a deep sleep many times thanks to a dream about Elle's naked body. He had been—for so long—consumed with the curiosity of what lay beneath her prim clothes.

Now, he didn't have to wonder. Now he knew. But he had a feeling she would still haunt his dreams.

No. Because you will have her until you are finished with her.

Yes, he would. Even if burning it out meant reducing them both to ash.

He stripped his suit jacked off and cast it onto the floor, spreading it as wide as he could. Then he swept her into his arms, and lay her down on the fabric.

He didn't have time to worry about anything. He was too needy. Too desperate. Two more things to add to her list of sins, because ever since he had made his fortune, ever since he had pulled himself up from poverty he had ensured he was never needy or desperate.

He pressed a kiss to her inner thigh and she shuddered. Then he kissed her again, gratified to feel her tremble beneath his lips as he moved closer and closer to the heart of her desire.

"I am desperate to taste you," he said.

She bit her lip, closing her eyes and turning away as he flicked his tongue where she most wanted it. "Apollo," she said, "you don't have to…"

He planted his palms firmly on the soft globes of her ass, pulling her more firmly up against his mouth, tasting her deeply in response to her protest. She wiggled beneath him, and he wasn't certain if she was trying to get away, or if she was trying to move herself closer.

Either way, he didn't care. Either way, he was going to get what he wanted.

He brought his hands into play, stroking her with his fingers, thrusting one deep inside of her, reveling in how slick, how ready she was for him.

She was sweet, like dessert. A flavor he had never realized he craved until he had her on his tongue. And now, he knew that this was the thing he had been missing. This was what he had craved all this time.

He stroked her deeply, adding a second finger to the first. And she shattered beneath him, her internal muscles tight around him as she shuddered out her release.

"Oh, Apollo," she said, leaving no doubt that she knew exactly who she was with. Leaving no doubt that she wanted him. No one else but him.

"Are you ready for me, *agape*?"

She didn't speak, she only nodded.

He freed himself quickly from his slacks, not bothering to undo the buttons on his shirt, not bothering to move his hands any lower than his hips. And he thrust inside of her, the breath hissing through his teeth as she closed around him.

Yes, restraint was for other men. For better men.

He was going to conquer. Conquer his desire, his rage.

He would seize what he wanted. The only question was why he hadn't done it sooner.

He brought his hips against hers, his pelvis coming into contact with her clitoris every time he thrust deep inside of her warm, willing body. And he was lost, lost in this, in her. In Elle. And he didn't give a damn that they were in an elevator, he didn't care that he was using her. Nothing mattered but this.

He gave himself over to it completely, lost himself in the rhythm of her body, the slow, slick glide of their flesh, the soft, sweet sounds she made. The words that poured from her lips, hoarse whispers begging him to continue. To take her harder, faster, just please, *please*.

Inside, he was begging himself to hold off on finding his pleasure. He didn't want to go over the edge without taking her with him.

He wanted to do more than that. He wanted her screaming. He wanted her just as lost, just as obsessed as he was. Just as desperate to burn out the flame before it consumed his entire being. Utterly. Irrevocably.

He refused to be alone in this, in this destructive obsession. He would destroy her along with him.

That thought crystallized, clear and sudden in his mind as his release washed over him in an uncontrollable, endless wave. And then beneath him, she arched her back, crying out her own pleasure, her fingernails digging into his back, even through the fabric of his shirt. And he relished the slight bite of pain that came with the unending onslaught of pleasure. It was the only thing rooting him to the earth. The only thing keeping even part of himself under control.

And as she shuddered out her release beneath him, as

he skinned his hands over her bare skin, he realized exactly what he would do.

He would have her until he was through with her. Would build her up as the public face of the company. And when the time was right, he would drop the blade on the guillotine.

He would remove her from her position as CEO, and with that final move, remove the St. James family from his life. Close the chapter forever.

He would not simply burn out their desire, he would destroy her along with it.

He leaned forward, brushing his lips against hers. "Now there, *agape*, I'm not so bad, am I?"

CHAPTER FOUR

ELLE HAD OPTED to keep her mouth shut from the time she had slowly collected her clothing off the floor of the elevator. She stayed silent as Apollo's driver took them to her apartment and all while she packed her bags, with Apollo looming in the corner of her apartment, until they made their trek to the airport and boarded his private jet.

She attempted to keep the awestruck expression off her face as she gazed around the aircraft. She knew that he was rich. She just hadn't quite realized that he was *private jet* rich. She had been raised in very fortunate circumstances but, even so, her father didn't own his own plane.

Well, he certainly wouldn't *now* even if he had before. Because of Apollo. And it would do well for her to remember that.

The problem was she did remember. While they had made love or…whatever it was you called what the two of them had done, she was aware of who he was. How much he had done to destroy her family's legacy.

Still she wanted him.

She felt… She felt completely and totally frazzled. Somehow, she had ended up kissing Apollo again. And the moment they touched, it didn't stop there. It never stopped there. It *couldn't*.

Apparently.

"Do you approve?" he asked, sinking into the plush leather chair next to one of the windows that looked out on the tarmac. "Or am I to take that expression to mean you are terrified of your surroundings? It's very difficult to say."

"I like the plane. I'm a little bit afraid of being alone at thirty thousand feet with you."

"Afraid you'll join the mile high club?"

Dammit, *yes*. "I think we can both agree that whatever has been going on between us is not a good idea."

"It's a terrible idea. Take your seat so that we can ready for takeoff."

She looked around, elected to sit in the chair farthest from his. "For the record, I still hate you."

"Oh, I'm well aware," he said. "I think that was what you screamed in my ear only a few hours ago. Oh, no, I think what you actually screamed was 'more' and 'harder.'"

"It isn't like you weren't complicit."

"Complicit. *Explicit*."

"What exactly is your goal here, Apollo?" she asked. She didn't trust him. Not one bit. She was not in a position to refuse his command that she fly with him to Greece. Neither did she entirely trust his explanation.

"That depends," he said, leaning back in his chair, his body all leashed power and tension. "Are you speaking of business—" his gaze raked over her body "—or pleasure?"

"I thought we both agreed that the pleasure angle is a poor one for the two of us to take."

"It is. It's a terrible idea, *agape*. We hate each other. As you have stated many times. Or, more to the point, *you* hate *me*. I have no such strong feelings about you."

"No," she said, her tone biting, "you don't feel anything for me or my father. You simply destroyed us for your own pleasure."

"Your father's company was hemorrhaging money long before I came by to deal with it."

"So why didn't you help him?"

"That's a complicated issue, Elle," he said, his words hard.

"I don't have any trouble understanding complexities. Go right ahead and explain."

"There is more between your father and I than you know."

"Enlighten me," she said, the words escaping through clenched teeth.

"Not now. But understand what I'm doing is for a bigger purpose."

"Your ego? Honestly, you're unbelievable. He gave you everything. He loved you best from the beginning," she said, voicing the words that she never had before. Words she had long believed. "And now you've betrayed him for money."

"Love," he spat. "What is love, Elle? Tell me that. Is it what your father feels for you? As he moves you around like a pawn, desperate to put you between me and his queen? Did he love me, or did he see me as another tool he could use? I don't put any stock in love. It has never done anything for me, so I will hardly defer to it now."

Her heart was pounding hard, her throat tight. And she knew what she wanted. She hated herself then, more than she had ever hated him. "What do you want from me?"

"In the short term? I intend to burn this thing out between us. A fire can't keep on forever, can it?"

"Are you suggesting we sleep together while we are away from New York?"

"I'm doing something much stronger than suggesting."

Rage turned to excitement, flickering at the center of her being and radiating outward. The idea of being with him again, of touching him again, made her hands shake. "I didn't realize you got off on coercing women into your bed."

"We both know I didn't have to coerce you into it at all. Also," he said, his tone pointed, "we have never made it to a bed."

The thought of being in bed with him seemed…luxurious. The chance to explore his body at her leisure, rather than finding herself at the mercy of the explosion that occurred between them every time they touched. The force of it propelled her, made it impossible for her to think, impossible for her to resist. What would it be like to make the *decision* to have him? To give herself all night to indulge in that long-held desire for him.

She had always wanted him. And she had hated him for it. She'd been so angry that he was so…untouched. So utterly uninterested. So she'd pushed at him, tried to make him angry if she couldn't make him want her. She'd taunted him. And finally, she'd decided to taunt him sexually.

She could remember very clearly choosing the smallest, brightest bikini she could possibly find—one that absolutely clashed with her red hair, but one she felt would get her the attention she desired—to try to catch Apollo's eye when he came home to the family estate over break.

He had approached her as she'd gotten out of the pool and she'd felt… Naked. Alive. Afraid. So she'd defaulted to her usual position.

She could remember turning to him, her lips curled. *They'll let anyone into the estate, won't they? How my family's standards have fallen over the years.*

His eyes had blazed then. With anger. And he'd grabbed hold of her arm. She hadn't been afraid, though. She'd been...electrified.

He had held her there, looked at her hard, and for one moment, one desperate moment, she had imagined that she had seen lust in his eyes. That she had seen interest. But then, he had released her and turned away, leaving her there as though nothing at all had happened.

But now, somehow, for some reason, he wanted her, too. *This is your chance. To put it behind you once and for all so that you can move on.*

"All right," she said, ignoring the thrill of excitement that shot through her. "I agree. We have to get back on proper footing so that we can deal with each other as business partners."

"You arc not my partner."

"Whatever. Terminology aside I am agreeing to the idea of an affair. But it has to stay a secret. Can you imagine the scandal? Me. Dating my wicked stepbrother who stole my family legacy after he wormed his way into my father's good graces."

"Of course. I have no interest in parading my intimate association with you in front of the world. As I already said."

His words, his *tone*, rankled. "I find it funny that you speak of it as though you find it distasteful. Of course *I* do. Everyone who moves in business circles fears you. I can see why I would want to disassociate from you. But not why you would wish to disassociate from me."

He arched a brow. "I have a type, Elle. It is not buttoned-up redheads. As you know, gentlemen prefer blondes. Or, in my case, scoundrels prefer blondes, brunettes or redheads so long as they're willing to part their thighs. I like women who know how to smile. Who know how to have fun. I do not like little harpies who claw at me even as they tear my clothes off."

"You like it when I claw at you."

Heat flared in his dark eyes and she took that as a win. "I consider this a unique circumstance."

She wanted to ask him why he thought heat was exploding between them the way it was. She wanted to ask him if it was ever like this for him and the other women he had sex with. But that would betray her inexperience. And that was something she wasn't willing to do. She wanted to protect her vulnerable places. Wanted to shield everything she didn't know from him.

That was an old defense, and one that she employed daily. She hated asking for help. Hated appearing ignorant.

Her father was a hard man, and she had always had the impression that he was standing by waiting for her to disappoint him. So she never let him see when she was floundering. Never let him detect one bit of uncertainty in her. She had wrapped herself so tightly in her ironed-on exterior, so careful to never show a wrinkle. She had difficulty letting go of it under any circumstances.

And if she was determined to never let her father see her sweat that went even more for Apollo.

That meant she couldn't ask the questions that were gnawing a hole inside of her. They would just have to go unanswered. It didn't matter anyway. Nothing was going to come from her association with Apollo. Nothing except freedom from the bizarre hold he had over her—and her life.

She had spent far too long being preoccupied with him. She would just be glad to have it handled.

And if she was a little bit…giddy over the thought of some time to deal with the attraction…well, that was normal. People acted ridiculous when it came to sex. History was filled with examples. Wars were started over sexual desire. She could hardly expect herself to be above the kind of insanity that captured almost all of humanity.

She spent the rest of the plane ride musing about restraint and dozing on and off while Apollo continued to work. Every time she opened her eyes and looked at where he was sitting, he was maintaining the same position, his focus never broken from his laptop, or the spreadsheets in front of him.

It was strange, watching him from across the darkened cabin. He had changed so much in the past few years. The lines on his face becoming more pronounced, as though each year had left a mark behind, evidence of the living he'd done.

And as a teenager, he had never worn a suit. He had always kept his hair slightly longer back then, too. Now it was cropped ruthlessly short, as though he was trying to look like he had sprung out of the ground a very conservative billionaire.

She wanted to find that boy again. Strip off the layers and layers he'd put over the person he'd been. The one she had… Well, the one she had felt so many things for.

She let her eyes flutter closed again, and when she opened them, they had landed in Greece. Customs and passports and the like were handled in an efficient manner involving people coming to them and apologizing for any delays. After that, they were ushered into a limousine, all their bags packed quickly into the trunk as they departed straight from the plane to the highway.

Athens was an incredible sprawl she hadn't accurately pictured in her mind. The rolling hills were capped with white, not from snow, but from the stone houses packed tightly together, flowing along with the landscape.

The downtown wasn't anything like the glass-and-steel jungle of Manhattan. Ancient structures mixed with more modern buildings, the history and heritage of the nation evident in the intricate stonework, the massive pillars and marketplaces scattered throughout.

"Where are we going?"

"I have a villa just outside the city."

"Of course you do," she said. "But I thought we were going to your offices?"

"We will. At some point. But some adjustments have been made to accommodate some of our new goals."

"Meaning what?" she asked, tearing her eyes away from the scenery to look at him.

"I don't think it's that difficult to guess."

They drove out of the city, winding up the steep, packed hillsides. They escaped the sprawl, moving to an area where trees were more plentiful. Where houses were a little bit less common. Until they reached the top of a completely vacant hill that overlooked the sea. There, behind a secure set of wrought-iron gates was a white stone house that was even more imposing than the St. James family estate in upstate New York.

"Is this your primary residence now?"

He lifted his shoulder. "As much as any place, I suppose. It is my home, after all."

"I *do* know that. You were born here. You left here when you were eight."

His focus sharpened. "Have you been reading unauthorized biographies?"

"No," she said. "I just paid attention when you used to speak around the dinner table. I used to know you, Apollo, as difficult as it is to remember back that far."

An emotion she couldn't put a name to flashed through

his eyes. "I did not realize such memories were worth saving."

"Know your enemy, and all of that."

"I suppose so."

The limousine pulled closer to the house, and the driver put the car into Park. Elle opened up her own door, stepping out and looking up at the house. To her, it looked like a lot of cubes of varying sizes stacked on top of each other, large windows on all sides looking out at the hills behind them, and the ocean before them.

"It doesn't seem like you're afforded very much privacy," she said.

"Are you concerned that the village will see you naked? Because make no mistake, most of the time spent in this house will be spent without clothes."

The dark, sensual promise should have frightened her, offended her. Instead, it excited her.

"The thought crossed my mind," she said. No point in playing the prude now. Not when he knew full well she wasn't.

"Never fear. I can tint the windows at the flick of a switch, and we won't even have to sacrifice the view. But good to know you are on the same page as I am."

"I have great concern for my modesty." And her sanity.

"Well, I hope you don't concern yourself much with it in my presence." He walked ahead of her, moving to the front of the house. "Our things will be brought in momentarily. Come, let me show you around."

She followed him inside, her heart hammering, her mouth suddenly dry. She didn't know what might happen next. If he was going to strip her of her clothing immediately and press her up against a wall again. And if he did, what would she do? She would capitulate. She knew that from experience.

But he didn't make a move to touch her. Instead, he paused in the expansive entryway. "I think this is self-explanatory," he said, indicating the living area with the low-profile couch that was up against the wall, curving around to another. "Beyond that is the pool." He walked ahead, up the open staircase that led to the second floor. She followed him. "My office," he said. "The library, kitchen and dining area. I felt the second floor made for a slightly better view." He continued straight up the stairs, to the third floor and she quickened her pace to keep up. "That way is my room," he said, pointing down to the left. "And then here you will find yours." The opposite direction from his. He began to walk to her room, and she followed, feeling a little bit like a lost puppy afraid of losing sight of her master.

He pushed the door open and revealed a light and airy space. Everything was white. The bedspread, the gauzy curtains that hung around the bed frame. There were no curtains on the windows, just as with the rest of the house. The square, unobstructed glass pane afforded a brilliant view of the jewel-bright sea, and let in the pale, sun-washed light.

"There are several settings for the windows. One is a blackout setting. That way the sun won't disturb your sleep," he explained.

She nodded. "I'm not sure I understand," she said, looking around the room. "I thought we would be sharing a room."

He chuckled. "I don't sleep with my lovers, *agape*. I have sex with them. We don't need to share a bedroom for that."

Dammit. He managed to make her feel completely gauche and out of her depth even though she was doing her best to appear like all of this was commonplace for her. She'd been feeling like she was succeeding. Until this moment. She gritted her teeth. "Of course. How could I be so silly?"

"I imagine you typically date nice boys who like to spend the evening making love before they pull you close and cuddle you."

His mocking tone burned her down deep. She was starting to feel at a disadvantage again. She would not allow it. "Do I seem like the type of woman who enjoys cuddling?" she asked, arching a brow. "You cannot possibly guess at the sort of man I typically associate with. You don't even know me. Not even a little bit. You know what I've bothered to show you, and that's all."

"My mistake. If you will excuse me, I'm going to get ready for this evening. And I have a bit of work to catch up on."

"You worked the entire time we were on the plane."

"Impatient for me?"

She swallowed hard. She swallowed her honest answer, which was most definitely yes. "Just concerned you're going to fall over at the age of twenty-nine from high blood pressure or something."

"Your concern is touching. I will see you this evening for the charity gala."

He turned and walked out of the room, closing the door behind him.

She turned and looked out the window, gazing at the view. For some reason, this time, she had the feeling of being inside of a terrarium, but it didn't feel quite so open. Once that thought entered her mind she felt as if she were some kind of creature he was keeping in a cage until he was ready to take her out and play with her.

Somehow, back in New York this had all felt equal, like they were in the same space, wanting the same things. But not now. Silly, because he owned her company. She should not have felt equal with him in the workplace. Should not have felt like they were on the same footing at all. And yet, for some reason—her pride, her intense dedication to her business persona—she had felt like they were.

But not here. In his house, in this show of his incredible wealth, she felt vulnerable. Powerless. She was in his home country, a place where she didn't even speak the language, trapped in his house on the hill.

She wondered, for a moment, if this was what he had felt. Walking into her family home as a teenager, his mother engaged to a powerful man so far above her station. And he had been greeted by a stepsister so consumed with her own feelings, her own issues, that she'd been nothing but horrible. Had done nothing but try to make him feel completely unequal to the place.

She blinked, pushing back an unwanted wave of sympathy. That was in the past. What she'd done had been out of girlish fear of the strength of her feelings.

Apollo was not acting as a boy, reacting to fear. He wasn't reacting at all. He was a man on the warpath, and God help her if she got in his way.

CHAPTER FIVE

WHEN ELLE APPEARED at the top of the stairs that evening wearing the silk gown that he'd had sent up to the room earlier, Apollo wasn't sure he had the strength to attend the gala. No, most of him wanted to grab hold of her and drag her straight into her bedroom and strip it off her.

The emerald green silk gown seemed almost demure in the front. It had a high neckline, the delicate, shiny fabric skimming her curves. It rippled when she walked down the stairs, flowing over her body like water.

But it was the back he couldn't wait to see. He had selected the dress for that very reason. True to his word, he was intent on raising her profile in the company. All the better to make her family's humiliation more apparent. If no one knew who the St. James family were, if they were only aware of the companies, while the family itself remained faceless, his disgrace of them would not carry the impact he required.

In a few weeks he would cut ties completely. He would let her drown along with her father and the rest of the St. James family.

It was cruel. But what David St. James had done to Apollo's father, the way he had manipulated Apollo's mother...

He forced himself to smile at her. To practice some

form of charm. He did possess it, after all. Though he didn't often exercise it when dealing with Elle. He could have any woman he wanted, and had, even before he had become the man he was now.

The girls he had associated with from nearby all-girls institutes back when he had been a teenager had found him fascinating. None of them had ever intended on taking him home to meet their parents. But a great many of them had taken him to nearby gazebos, backseats of cars and vacant dorm rooms. He might not be the kind of man they could proudly claim, but they had certainly found him attractive enough for certain uses.

Of course, Elle had already proven she had no issues using him for her physical satisfaction while she despised him on a personal level. So, he supposed that there was no point in attempting to be charming now.

All thoughts of charm or anything else were completely emptied from his mind when he saw the side of the gown as she reached the bottom of the stairs. He could think of nothing more than the possibility of stripping it from her body now.

"Turn around," he said, his voice hard.

"Why?" she asked, turning to face him, her hands clasped in front of her, demure, as though she had no idea what she was doing to him.

"Turn around," he said, deciding that he would forgo charm completely.

A flash of color spread up her neck, into her cheeks. Clearly, even if it made her angry, she quite enjoyed it when he gave orders. She turned slowly, teasing him by taking her time. And when she revealed her back fully, his stomach tightened, his blood pooling in his groin.

The back of the dress was a deep V ending just above the curve of her rear, exposing her entire back, the edges glittering with delicate beadwork. The seams over the silken material served to enhance the round shape of her backside, creating an even more dramatic shape to her curves.

He wanted to take her back upstairs, not just so he could have his way with her, but so he could keep any other man from laying eyes on what he thought of as his.

"It does not matter how many men have come before me," he said, not realizing he was speaking the words out loud until they had already escaped his mouth. "You are mine now. You have always been mine, Elle." The words were more raw, more real than he'd intended.

But then, this feeling was more raw, more real than anything that had ever come before it.

He saw attachments for what they were. Saw clearly how easily feelings could be manipulated. But what he felt for Elle was beyond him. It could never be distilled into one neat emotion. Could hardly ever be defined.

He needed it gone. Needed to burn it out. So that in the end he could walk away from the St. James family and never look back.

Walk away from her.

She turned to face him, her signature red ponytail swinging along with the movement. "That's quite possessive," she said.

"I'm kind of a bastard. You have agreed to be my mistress until such time as we have burned out the attraction between us. That means you are mine. And mine alone."

"I hardly make a habit of overlapping lovers."

He took a step toward her, closing the distance between them. He wrapped his arm around her waist, planting his hand firmly at the center of her back and drawing her close to him. "I would not permit it."

"You might own my company, Apollo," she said, her voice low, sultry, "but you do not own me."

"That's where you're wrong, I think," he said, sliding his hand up the center of her back, cupping the back of her head. "Because for now those two things are the same. I own both the company and you."

"You're a caveman."

He wrapped his fingers around her ponytail, tugging hard. "Shall I drag you back to my lair?"

She gasped, the sound one of arousal, not fear.

"You can pretend to hate this thing between us all you want. You can pretend to hate my commands. But we both know that no matter how shocked and appalled you pretend to be, you want this. You want me."

She leaned in slightly, and he kept his hold tight on her hair. Then she pressed her lips gently against his before biting him hard. "I might want you," she said, "but it is not the way a woman *should* want a man."

"Take your hair down."

"I refuse to give in to your every command."

He shifted his hold on her, grabbing the bobby pin that was buried in the ponytail that wrapped one coppery strand around the rubber band that secured her hair, concealing it from view. Then he grabbed the rubber band itself, pulling it free.

Her red hair fell past her shoulders in soft waves, extra full because of the way it had been restrained.

She frowned, her brows locked together. "I can't go like this. My hair is a mess."

"It is perfect."

"I do not have to wear my hair to please you."

"Your hair pleases me however it is fixed," he said. "But this way, this way, all I can think about is burying my fingers in it. Pulling you toward me. Kissing you deeply. With it like this, I want nothing more than to take you straight back upstairs and make you scream my name. And so, I leave the final decision on how you wear it up to you."

She tilted her chin upward. "Well, it's already down."

He chuckled, the soundboard of satisfaction. "I thought you might come to that conclusion."

She narrowed her eyes. "I prefer you without a tie."

"It is a formal event."

"Without the black tie, with the first button on your shirt undone, so that I can just see your chest hair, all I can think of is you tearing the shirt open the rest of the way so that I can put my hands on your hard muscles. So that I can feel your heartbeat raging against my palms. I can think of nothing but leaning in, running my tongue over your skin. And so," she said, arching her brow before turning away from him. "It is up to you."

Apollo smiled and began to loosen his tie.

No matter that they were pretending to be merely business associates at the gala, Elle could not help but think the two of them looked like they had been engaged in sexual intimacy in the car on the way. Her hair was down, looking very much like he had already run his fingers through it. His shirt was undone, his tie long discarded.

And yet, they had not had the benefit of engaging in any kind of intimate activity.

When they had gotten in the limousine she had scooted as far away from him as possible, telling him she needed space, time to collect her thoughts. She did. She was exhausted, jet-lagged, and the nap she'd had earlier had only helped a little bit. Beyond that, she was still raw from their last encounter. And if they were supposed to appear in public together in a platonic fashion, she did not want the feeling of his touch lingering quite so strongly in the forefront of her mind.

Now though, she was regretting it. Now she sort of wished she had climbed onto his lap in the car and satisfied her desire for him. Anything to take the edge off the extreme arousal that was pounding through her even now.

The gala itself was beautifully appointed, held in one of the oldest and most sophisticated hotels in Athens. When she arrived, she was surprised to see that Apollo's name was on everything.

"You didn't tell me that it was *your* charity gala we were attending."

He shrugged his shoulder, taking a glass of Champagne off the tray of a passing waiter. "It did not seem important."

"I think it is rather important. I wasn't aware that you had founded the charity."

"It's very boring. Press junket stuff. The kind of thing that one says to improve their reputation with the media. It's a game I scarcely have the patience to play at the best of times. I did not see the point in trying to convince you that I was somehow a paragon of virtue simply because I donate money to impoverished families."

"You do?" In spite of everything she knew about him, in spite of her feelings about him, she could feel herself softening.

"Yes. Do not look at me like that. I am a businessman. Believe me when I tell you this benefits me in financial ways."

"Why are you so resistant to being seen as good in any fashion?"

"I do not like to raise people's expectations."

She blinked. "Why?"

"Because they will find themselves disappointed."

She looked around, taking in the beautifully appointed marble interior of the hotel, the impressive pillars, the glittering chandeliers. Couples dressed in the finest couture were already making their way out to the dance floor. She wished she could dance with Apollo. That he would take her into his strong arms and pull her up against his chest, hold her...just to hold her. So that she could relish his strength, his heat, if only for a moment.

She shook her head. That was extreme foolishness. She wanted nothing more from Apollo than for him to leave her alone and allow her to run their business as she saw fit. Well, that and sex for the sake of sex, until they had burned out the attraction between them.

She did not want him to hold her. She did not want to press her head up against his chest and listen to the sound of his heart. Did not want to spend an hour kissing him, just kissing him. *No*, she didn't want any of those things.

"I shall introduce you to some of my associates," Apollo said. "And to some of the members of the press who are in attendance."

"Oh, you're too kind," she said, keeping her tone light.

He pressed his hand lightly on her back, guiding her toward a group of people who were standing there conversing. He made introductions, and dropped his hand quickly back to his side, bringing a great deal of distance between the two of them as he shifted his position within the group.

One of the men was a businessman from Italy, another a Greek, who had his business in the United States. They started to make conversation about staying relevant in the age of the internet and online superstores, and she was so lost in the discussion that it took her a while to notice that

Apollo was no longer standing next to her. She frowned, searching the crowd quickly. And then she spotted him, out on the dance floor with a blonde woman wearing a dress with a hem that fell just beneath her butt cheeks. Rather nice butt cheeks too, Elle was loath to admit.

She fought to keep the scowl off her face. She knew that they were supposed to be playing the part of business associates but she felt this was taking it a bit far.

"I see Mr. Savas has abandoned you," the Greek man, Nikos Vardalos, said.

"Not at all," she said, taking a deep breath. "We are not here together. Mr. Savas is able to dance with whoever he chooses."

"Then I suppose you are free to dance with whoever you choose?"

She could always tell him she had a boyfriend. She often did that when confronted with men she wasn't attracted to in these kinds of situations. But Nikos was handsome enough, and Apollo was dancing with someone else. Really, it seemed rather silly for her to stay hidden away in a corner.

"Absolutely," she said. "I am always free to do whatever I want."

He laughed, treating her to a smile that she had no doubt often made women go weak in the knees. Sadly, not her. Not now.

But she pretended. She offered a smile in return.

"I like a woman who knows her mind. And does your mind tell you that you might want to dance with me?"

"I would be delighted."

He extended his hand, and she accepted it, wrapping her fingers around his. His touch was warm, but it did not light her on fire, not the way that Apollo's did. It was sort of comforting, to have a man touch her like this, and for her to feel so very little.

Every interaction with Apollo, every brush of his skin against hers, was so layered. Was so hot, so intense, she couldn't ignore it, or pretend it hadn't burned. It was never simple. It was always hate spread over lust, spread over a strange attachment that stemmed from all of the years they had known each other. And betrayal. The betrayal that was unique to what she felt for him because of how well they had known each other. Because of how she had felt about him for so long.

Because of the way she had trusted him.

And you betray your father by sleeping with this man. By wanting him.

Still, she couldn't help herself. Still, she could feel nothing as Nikos pulled her into his arms and swept her onto the dance floor. Still, she felt more when she looked across the crowded room and locked eyes with Apollo, who was glaring at her and her dance partner with dark rage.

Fine. He was welcome to be murderous. She didn't particularly care. They were here separately. He was dancing with another woman, and she would be damned if she would play the part of wallflower.

She shifted her hands lightly on her partner's shoulder, tightening her grip on his hand.

"I think Savas wants to kill me," Nikos said, his tone tinged with amusement.

"Oh, I don't suppose he wants to kill you," she said, her tone dry. "Anyway, he and I are associates, as I said before. And neither of us believes in mixing business with pleasure."

"Excellent. Then I shall never do business with you."

She laughed. "Well, that would be a shame. Since

you are in retail, I would very much like to do business with you."

"Perhaps it is crass of me to discuss this during a dance," he said, "but tell me more."

They spent the next two songs largely ignoring the music and discussing the various ways in which they could marry their two brands. She decided that she liked Nikos quite a bit even if he did not make her heart beat faster.

She only wished that he could.

He was Greek, he was wealthy, he had a hint of a gorgeous accent. Truly, if she had a type, this was it. If any other man was going to start a fire in her loins quite the way that Apollo did, this man would. But there was nothing. Absolutely nothing. It was an extreme disappointment.

Still, though she had not found a way to encourage desire toward another man, she had come away with a very promising business contact. They parted at the end of the song, and he did not try to make any sort of romantic overture. He must've sensed the lack of chemistry as profoundly as she did.

She was making her way toward a waiter to get herself a drink when she was all but accosted by Apollo. "Having fun?"

"It's a charming party," she said.

"Yes. I told you already that you would be with me and me alone while we work out the attraction between us, did I not?"

"I'm sorry, I was not aware that a waltz was on par with intercourse."

"You are playing with fire," he said.

"Then you are, too. Don't think I didn't notice your lovely blonde partner."

"It is expected of me."

"And you want my face in the paper. Therefore, I had better do something newsworthy. You put me in this dress that leaves me essentially naked, and now you're going to act as though my getting attention is not somehow essential to your *plan*?"

"All you have to do is simply walk into a room to gain attention, *agape*. Trust me on this."

"I find your assessment flattering, if slightly ambitious."

"I don't care whether or not you find it ambitious. It is the truth." He looked around them. "Even if you have not noticed, I have. Every male eye—and many of the female eyes—have been on you from the moment you walked in. You are absolutely the one to watch here."

"Is that so?"

"Yes. And when you make a large charitable donation in the name of the company, you will become even more of a conversation piece."

Her mouth opened, then snapped shut. "I did not know you were going to make use of my money."

"Of course I am. Anyway, it is a good cause, on that you can trust me. As I said, I provide housing and other necessities for families who have fallen below the poverty line. Surely you can find no fault with that."

"I suppose not."

"You sound so distressed. It must be terrible when I don't rise to the part of blackguard when it suits you."

"Sincerely awful. I can see why you prefer to pretend you're terrible. For consistency."

"I am nothing if not consistent."

She laughed. "If only that were true."

"What is that supposed to mean?"

"Exactly what it sounds like. You are not consistent,

I don't care how you frame it, I don't care what you say. You were a friend of my family, and then you betrayed us. There is nothing consistent about that."

His expression turned dark, fierce. He leaned in and her breath caught in her throat. She thought, for a moment, that he might kiss her. She hoped that he would. He did not. "From the moment I understood there was better than the circumstances I existed in I was determined to find better. When I went to a private school, knowing full well that I didn't belong there, I was determined to rise to the top of the class so that no one could question whether or not I had the ability to succeed in the realms of society into which I had been thrust. I have done nothing but hold myself up from the bottom with my brute strength from the moment I understood it could be done. If that's not consistency, I don't know what is."

"Yes, I know you pulled yourself up quite a bit. But it's quite convenient to forget that my father's money provided a ladder to help you out." She turned away from him and he grabbed hold of her arm, holding on tightly to her and pulling her back to him.

"I was willing to advance myself using any means necessary. Again, I claim consistency." He released his hold on her, straightening the cuffs on his shirt. "Go off and have fun. We will meet again at the end of the night. Do not forget to make your donation."

"Of course not."

"I imagine Luka would like to dance, as well."

"Are you off to find him?" she asked.

"No, but I suggest you should."

"Now you're encouraging me to dance with other men? There's that legendary consistency."

"No, I believe you're right. You should do what you

can to get your photograph in the news. And I shall do what I have to to get attention of my own. I will see you at the end of the evening."

CHAPTER SIX

BY THE TIME the car pulled back up to Apollo's house later that evening he was in a violent temper. Elle had done exactly as he had demanded and had danced with every businessman within fifteen years of her age. And she had charmed every single one of them. She had no doubt delighted the media.

She had done exactly as he'd asked, and he was incensed. Spending the evening *not* touching her had been akin to torture. But he was ready to move ahead with their agreement. He was ready to claim her. To remind her exactly why she was here, and who she was with.

They had not spoken in the car on the way back to his villa. She was vibrating with indignation next to him, but he didn't care.

When they got out of the car and walked into the house he turned to her. "I want you to go to your room and open up the top drawer of the bureau there. You will find some other items that my staff has procured for you. Make yourself ready for me."

He stormed off to his office then, pouring himself a glass of scotch and downing it in one desperate gulp, relishing the burn as it slid down his throat.

He paced the length of the room, trying to figure out exactly what happened to make him so agitated.

Jealousy.

He could not remember the last time he had ever felt jealous. If he ever had.

He closed his eyes, allowing an old memory to wash over him. Hell, the bikini. Yes, he had been jealous then in a strange way. Of the fact that she was young, with her entire life ahead of her. Of the fact that men had not yet discovered her, and he would not be a part of that discovery. He would have given everything to have been the first man to touch her. To have been the one to awaken her sensuality. Her every sigh, her every moan.

To have been the one who gave her that first climax.

Yes, he would have given anything to be that man at one time. He had been jealous then. Of a man who had not existed. And somehow tonight every man who had danced with her had become one of those nameless, faceless men who had come before him.

He hated them, even without knowing who they were.

He tossed his suit jacket onto the floor, stalking out of his office and going up the stairs toward her bedroom. She had better damn well be ready for him. Because he was not waiting another moment.

He threw open the bedroom door without knocking, and she turned to face him, still wearing the dress she had been wearing to the gala.

"I thought I gave you instructions to change," he said.

Her green eyes glittered with anger. "Yes," she said. "You did. But I have no desire to dress up like some strange interpretation of a fantasy that you have, brought about by your magnanimous staff."

"Expensive underthings offend you?"

"The idea that I might not want to choose my own? The idea that I might be interchangeable with any of the other women you consort with? That offends me."

"What do any of my other lovers have to do with this?"

"Everything. You are treating me exactly as you would any of them."

He clenched his hands into fists, his heart beating so fast it burned. "And you want to be special? Is that it?"

Her cheeks flamed. "I don't want to be the same. I don't want to be just one warm body of any of the ones you could have."

"Still you doubt my desire for you?" He undid another button on his shirt, then another, stripping it off as he walked toward her, feeling every inch a predatory animal. "What must I do to show you that I am your servant, *agape*? What must I do to show you that you own my body?"

The color heightened in her cheeks. "I own your body?"

"Do you think I want this? Do you think I want to be a slave to the desire I have for a St. James? If you think you hate me then just imagine how much I hate you. Your family. Your family name. Everything you stand for."

His words were coming out hard and fast. He was saying more than he had intended. He had never intended to bring this up with her at all. Had not intended to speak any of this to her until he was giving her her marching orders and ordering her to pack her things and vacate her office. He had not intended to reveal any of this until he'd unleashed his ultimate betrayal on to her.

But he couldn't stop it now. He could not stop himself. "If any woman at the party tonight had made me feel even a fraction of what I feel for you I would have taken her into the nearest hallway and pushed her skirt up. Sadly, I only respond to you. You have me on a leash, Elle. I hope you are happy with this revelation."

Her eyes were round, her lips parted slightly. "I don't

understand. You were part of our family. How can you possibly feel that way?"

"Easily. You don't understand what manner of man your father is, you don't understand what manner of man I am. When you were seventeen years old, parading around the family estate in your bikini, I would have liked nothing more than to put you flat on your back. I was a man of twenty, and I would have had you, sweet little virgin that you were. And even knowing how wrong that is, I hate every man who came before me. I regret not taking you then. Such wasted years, Elle. I could have rid myself of my hunger for you then. But I didn't. For what reason? To preserve some semblance of a conscience we both know I don't have? Pointless. But then, I still harbored illusions that I might be good."

"I… You wanted me then?"

"Did you not know? Of course not. You were blind. A little virgin."

"Stop saying that. I wasn't ignorant. It's just that you seemed angry…not…"

"As it always is with us."

"Either way, I'm not ignorant."

"Did I have the wrong end of it then? Please don't tell me you weren't already experienced or I truly will hang myself for being so foolish that I didn't have you."

"Why are you acting like this?"

He didn't know. He damn well had no clue. All he knew was that he was enraged. Over tonight. The other men who'd touched her. The orders she was refusing to obey. Over his behavior nine years ago. Over his behavior now. "Why are you refusing to wear the lingerie I provided for you?"

"Because I will not be one of your whores," she said. "Because I *was* a virgin when you had me at your hotel room. Your jealousy is misplaced while mine is certainly not."

Her words hit him like a punch to the gut. "A virgin?"

"Apparently it matters to you. Apparently you are quite proprietary and possessive, though you have not earned the right to be."

He growled, pulling her into his arms, grabbing hold of the sides of the delicate fabric of the dress and wrenching it down over her shoulders, tugging the bodice down low, revealing her breasts to his hungry gaze. "I am the only man to ever have you?"

"Yes," she said, her voice breathless.

"This pleases me much more than it should," he said, gripping her chin between his thumb and forefinger and tilting her face up to him. "All during the ride back to the villa I was contemplating the different ways I could kill each and every man who danced with you. In my mind, they had become your previous lovers. And I discovered that I felt rather violent about them. About the missed opportunity I'd had. You see, I wanted to be the one to teach you about pleasure."

She bit her lip, as though she were holding back a litany of words. Either curses, or the confirmation that he had indeed been the one to teach her about pleasure. He had a feeling she neither wanted to yell at him at this moment nor give him anything pleasant to latch onto.

"I did teach you about pleasure, didn't I? Against the wall in a hotel room. Dammit, Elle, you didn't tell me."

"Would it have made a difference?"

No. It made no difference at all. Not to anything. Not to what had gone before, and not to what he must do now. The fact that Elle had been a virgin changed nothing. She had been innocent of the wrongdoings of her father before he knew that, and she was innocent of them now. The fact he was her only lover might fill him with a sense of masculine pride, a sense of conquest, but it didn't change the fact that he would betray her in the end. That he would make an example of her and use her to wound her father.

The way her father had wounded his father. The way he had devastated his mother. The way he had devastated Apollo himself.

Whatever sins his father had committed, the rest of them had been nothing more than collateral damage. And so would Elle be. It was not fair. But none of this was fair.

It wasn't about fairness. It was about justice in the way that only he could obtain it.

"Yes," he lied. "It would have made a difference. I would have been much gentler with you." Except he knew he would not have. He would not take that fiery encounter in the hotel room back for anything. When Elle had unleashed all her rage on him. All of her desire. It had been the most singular experience of his life. He would trade it for nothing. It was a moment that belonged to him, one that could not be stolen no matter how low he sunk.

He was a villain, and now, he was embracing it fully.

He leaned in, kissing her, keeping it soft, keeping it light. She grabbed hold of his face, deepening the kiss.

He picked her up, carrying her to the bed and laying her down on the soft mattress, tugging the gown from her body. There would be no more talking tonight.

If he had his way, there would be no more talking until he was through with her. And if that meant spending the next two weeks in bed, then they would spend the next two weeks in bed.

CHAPTER SEVEN

THE PAST TWO weeks at Apollo's villa had gone surprisingly smoothly. It was strange to coexist with him and not fight. It actually reminded Elle of a different time. A simpler time. Back when they had actually liked each other. When she had looked up to him. When he had—apparently—had some sort of attraction to her that he had buried.

Of course, maybe they had coexisted so peacefully because their lives had been essentially separate. Unless they were making love. Which had not been confined to evenings, or to bed. She was certain that at this point, Apollo had taken her on every surface in the entire villa.

She was not complaining. It had been... Well, it had been the culmination of her most heated fantasies. It was strange. Like she was living a life borrowed, one that she could not possibly have in the long term, but one that was in many ways preferable to the one she had been living. She was still seeing to her responsibilities. Sometimes working in his office, sometimes from the office in his home while he was out.

She couldn't complain about the vacation. Of course, it was also difficult to justify the fact that she was sleeping with the enemy. Though, not literally, since they didn't sleep together. They had sex, and then he left.

"It's how I do things, *agape*," she said, amusing herself with her poor imitation of Apollo's voice as she paced the length of her bedroom.

A knock on her bedroom door startled her. She wondered if she had summoned him just by thinking about him. But he had just gone out to work a couple of hours ago, so she doubted he was back already.

She opened the door, to see one of his servants, Maria, standing there holding a package. "This is for you, miss," she said.

"Oh," she said, her whole body getting warm when she realized what it was. "Thank you."

After Maria left, she closed the door and opened the package hurriedly. Inside was a hot pink bikini. She had been planning this for the past few days. Maybe it was juvenile. But she wanted a chance to recapture the moment that both of them had missed. One that seemed to linger in both their minds.

She didn't waste any time getting into it, examining herself in the full-length mirror, watching as her cheeks flooded with color. She didn't make a habit out of wearing things that were so revealing. Though, honestly, after spending so much time naked with Apollo, she shouldn't feel self-conscious.

Still, she did.

That was different. That all happened during the heat of the moment. This was…premeditated. She had never staged anything quite like a seduction with him. And that's what this was. But she was aching for something, searching for something more. She couldn't deny that what she felt for him wasn't hatred at this point. It would be so much easier if it was.

She felt… Well, she felt a lot.

She took a deep breath, opening her bedroom door

and heading down the hall, down the stairs and outside to the pool. She was intent on being there when he got back. Intent on giving him the chance to make a different decision this time when he saw her in the bathing suit.

She slipped beneath the warm water, paddling over to the edge of the infinity pool, looking out over the view of the ocean. It was beautiful here. She hadn't thought it was possible to feel so at peace in Apollo's lair. Certainly not when she had first arrived.

She couldn't say they were growing closer, not exactly. But…it was more than it had been. For one thing, they could be in each other's presence for a full five minutes without screaming at each other. Sometimes they could go that long without tearing each other's clothes off, too. But only sometimes.

The thought made her smile, she lifted her face up to the sky, bathing herself in the warmth of the sun.

"What are you doing out here?"

"I finished work early," she said, turning, her heart slamming hard against her breastbone when she saw Apollo standing there, still dressed in the suit that he'd worn to work.

"Come here," he said, his jaw set, his dark eyes intent on her.

Elle draped her arms over the back of the infinity pool, arching her back slightly, thrusting her breasts up out of the water. "I'm enjoying the water."

"Elle," he said, his tone warning. "Do not make me come in there and get you."

"I think I would like for you to come in and get me. It's what you should have done nine years ago."

He smiled, a genuine smile. It wasn't one that was tinged with cynicism, neither was it mocking or laden with barely contained rage. It made her heart turn over in her chest, made it expand.

He began to remove his suit, starting with his jacket, then his tie, then slowly undoing the buttons on his shirt. There had been ample time over the past couple of weeks for her to become familiar with that gorgeous male physique, but familiarity hadn't made him seem commonplace. Not in the least.

He arched a brow, slowly placing his hands on his belt buckle, working the leather through the loop. Her mouth went dry and she fought to keep herself from moving closer to him. She was going to hang back. She was going to force him to come to her.

He undid the closure on his slacks, pulled the zipper down slowly, his eyes never leaving hers. He pushed his pants down his narrow hips, exposing himself to her. He was everything. Absolute perfection. Everything she had wanted a man to be and then some. No, there was no chance of him ever becoming commonplace in her eyes.

Slowly, he made his way to the pool, climbing down, the water rising up and concealing his body from her.

"You took my show," she said, just as he leaned forward, his sleek, athletic body slicing through the water effortlessly.

"I thought I would bring it to you," he said, approaching her, wrapping his arm around her waist and drawing her up against him.

"Oh," she said, "I guess I can appreciate that."

"I think you can more than appreciate that," he said, looking pointedly down at her breasts, at her tightened nipples, pushing up against the thin fabric of the bathing suit.

"I make it too easy for you," she said, not sounding even remotely regretful.

"I'm not complaining," he said, sliding his hand down her waist, resting his hand on her butt.

"Of course you're not. You're so certain of yourself, and all I have done is make you even more certain."

"I was named after a god. I came into the world with a rather inflated view of myself."

"Of course you did. How could I forget?" She lifted her hand, resting her palm on his chest. "I ordered this bathing suit for you."

Heat illuminated the darkness in his eyes. "I thought you might have."

"We have a chance to make a different decision." She traced the water droplets that were trailing down his chest, rolling into the grooves of his muscles. "I wish that I had done something differently then. Been a little bit bolder."

"You were young. You shouldn't have done anything. I shouldn't have done anything."

"I was young, but I knew what I wanted. And it hasn't changed." She looked up at him. "I still want you. I wanted you all this time, even when I was angry at you."

He wrapped his fingers around her wrist, lifting her hand to his lips, pressing a kiss to her palm. "Yes, I know you did. Believe me when I say the feeling is mutual."

Those words, those husky, delicious words, sent a little shock of pleasure through her. It wasn't strictly physical. It went deeper than that.

Unfortunately, all of this went much deeper than the physical. Much deeper than she wanted it to go.

"I do."

A smile curved his wicked mouth. "Listen to us. We have managed to converse for several minutes without fighting."

"A miracle."

"Perhaps. Though, I imagine we are skirting the edge of sacrilege assigning anything divine to the nature of things between us."

"Perhaps."

He had a point. What they shared was carnal, lustful.

No, not only that. Beautiful. Altering.

Impossible.

He was her stepbrother, he was her enemy. Truly, it was the enemy part that made it most impossible. The stepbrother issue would hardly mean anything. They hadn't been raised together. They shared no blood.

There's no affection, either. Not from him.

She squeezed her eyes shut, unable to look at him while she had thoughts like that. He closed the distance between them, pressing his lips against hers. And she just let it wash over her, warmer than the sun, more refreshing than the water they were standing in.

Desire assaulted her, her stomach tightening, a pulse beating low and hard at the apex of her thighs.

It had been just over a month since their first encounter in his hotel room in New York. Just over a month since she'd been with a man for the first time. It hadn't taken long for her to grow accustomed to it. For her to know exactly what she wanted. For her to learn his body, and to learn what hers desired of him.

He slipped his hand beneath her bikini bottoms, taking hold of her with his large palm. She loved his hands. Loved the feel of them on every inch of her. Loved looking at them. Spent a great deal of time fantasizing about them.

But then, it was like that with every single inch of him.

So many things did not live up to the promise. Did not live up to the hype. Apollo was not one of them. He took her every fantasy and superseded by leaps and bounds.

In comparison with the reality her fantasies of what sex with him would be like seemed childish. Simple.

She had known it would feel good, she had known she would find him attractive. She hadn't realized it would be so raw, so exposing. Hadn't realized it would strip her bare of everything, not just her clothes. She had thought it would just be physical.

That was such a simplistic thought. His body was the missing piece of hers. He was everything she ached for in the dead of night, the reason that she felt hollow sometimes. It was because she was desperate to have him inside of her. Only him.

She parted her lips for him, expecting him to conquer, expecting him to invade. Instead, he was gentle, his tongue sliding slowly against hers, the slick glide sending a sharp pang of need through her. So acute it was almost painful.

She forked her fingers through his hair, deepening the kiss, pressing her body as firmly against his as she could. She knew that if any of his staff members walked out now they would get a bit of a show. But honestly, her brain was too foggy with desire to really get a handle on that reality. She couldn't care. Not for her modesty, not for anyone's sensibilities. There was only this. Only him.

She lost all sense of propriety, all sense of loyalty, all sense of…everything when she was with him.

She became a new person. A different version of Elle.

She had to wonder what might have happened if she had taken the steps to close the distance between them nine years ago. If they would have forgotten about decency back then.

It didn't matter. They were doing this now. She tried to shove aside the thoughts of everything else that had happened in the ensuing years. The wedge that had been driven into the family.

Her father, his mother and her, all on one side of the gulf, with him on the other.

She didn't want to think about them. Not now. Didn't want to think about the father she could never be good enough for. The father who had preferred her stepbrother to her.

Probably still did, in truth. Even though Apollo had taken a chunk out of David St. James's empire, he probably privately celebrated his stepson's ruthlessness.

Apollo might have betrayed them. But Apollo never acted like he wished she were someone else. Apollo never made her feel like she wasn't good enough. He gloried in her body, in the attraction between them. It was more than she had ever had from...anyone.

The thought filled her with a sudden, intense swell of emotion. Whatever they had, whatever this was, it fed her soul in a way nothing else did. Because it was about her. It wasn't about the business. It wasn't about performing to his satisfaction. He cared about performing to hers. They were in this together. They wanted each other.

For once she wasn't striving for approval. Wasn't trying to live up to an expectation she simply never could.

Her father had seen Apollo as his hope. The son he never had. The heir she could never be.

Then he had trusted Apollo to bail him out, never speaking to her about anything. Never consulting her. He had always trusted Apollo above her.

And Apollo had betrayed him.

But that didn't stand in the way of her and Apollo. He didn't look at her and see the unfulfilled promises of someone else. He wanted her. In spite of everything.

It was balm for her soul.

He swept her into his arms, lifting her as though his arms were created to cradle her close. As though she was the perfect weight and size for him. As though this moment had been fated from the beginning.

He carried her up from the pool, striding right into the house, clearly just as unconcerned as she was about being seen. She had a feeling his staff was paid to look the other way when he was conducting affairs in his home. She shoved that thought to the side. She wasn't going to think about other times, other women.

Right now, she was the only one. That would have to be enough.

He started up the stairs, and she put her hand on his cheek, tracing the fine lines on his face. Additions to his features, new and fascinating. She remembered his face so clearly as a teenage boy. Smooth, pretty. Full perfect lips, amusement in his dark eyes, a kind of irreverent quirk to his brow.

He was no longer smooth. Dark stubble covered his jaw, his chin. Deep grooves bracketed his mouth, marred his forehead. The face that had once been pretty was now more rugged, more distinguished. The laughter in his eyes was gone, replaced with a kind of intensity that burned her from the inside out.

The irreverence was still there, though. It was one of her favorite parts of him. That dry, sardonic humor that would make her laugh in the strangest moments. That would take her from anger to entertainment in only a few moments. That would see her kissing him instead of screaming at him thanks to one well-timed comment.

He was one of the few men who had ever stood up to her. Who had gone toe to toe with her and made her feel like she just might lose.

Not for the first time she wondered at the ground

they had covered since then. Wondered about what had happened.

But she didn't have time to turn it over anymore, because they had reached the top of the stairs, and only a second later, her bedroom.

He set her down, water dripping down her body, pooling down around her feet. "I'm going to get the carpet wet."

"I can't say I am very concerned about that."

"Well, it's your carpet."

"Yes, it is," he said, one side of his mouth curving upward.

He regarded her for a moment before taking a step toward her, tracing the line down the edge of her bikini top, the tip of his finger only barely delving beneath. "This is the stuff of my darkest fantasies."

"A fluorescent bikini?"

He chuckled. "You. In this bikini. So much of that beautiful, pale skin on display. Your hair... It should look ridiculous with this color. Instead, you're simply everything bright. I wanted you then. I consider this my reward for good behavior." His smile turned wicked. "You know, I only wish I had known you were a virgin."

"Is that so?"

"Yes. Had I known you were a virgin I would have relished my prize all the more. I was obsessed with having you first. With teaching you about pleasure."

"You did," she said. She had held the words back from him two weeks ago. Because she had not been ready to share that with him. Had not been ready to confess just how much he had meant to her. What it had meant that he was her first lover.

Or why he was.

But there was no use in protecting herself now. She didn't want to.

"It was always you that I wanted," she said. "That was why even though I said I hated you, even though I was so angry at you the first time I kissed you, it went as far as it did. Because it was always you for me, Apollo. No matter how many years have passed, no matter what ugly words were spoken between us, it was always you."

Apollo knew he did not deserve the words that Elle had just spoken. He was using her. For these past two weeks he had been using her. To satisfy his need for her. Biding his time until he could get his revenge, filling the hours with the pleasures of her body knowing that in the end he would betray her.

There was nothing else to do. This thing between them could not last. And he could not deviate from his course of revenge against his stepfamily. Not now.

He had made up his mind. There would be wreckage. Collateral damage.

But he wouldn't think of it now. Instead, he would take that unearned compliment. Savor it. Hold it close. He would consider this the satisfaction of a desire born years ago. The revenge would be a satisfaction of a different desire, but it was a separate issue. In his mind, she wasn't a St. James. Not now. Now, she was his lover. As he had long fantasized.

When he was finished he would end his association with her and continue on, viewing her again as the daughter of his enemy, rather than his mistress.

He could barely tear his gaze away from her, away from her pale, delectable curves, so effortlessly displayed by the flimsy material of the bikini.

That she had done this for him... It was strange. It

created a shifting sensation at the center of his chest, made him feel as though the earth had tilted slightly. This shared memory that they had of this time when they had wanted the same things… It was strange to have it here in the present.

Just take it. It is a gift.

He would. Whether he deserved it or not. Because, as he had already told her, he was the villain here. Nothing would change that.

Slowly, ever so slowly, he untied the top of the bikini, peeling it away from her luscious breasts, baring them to his gaze. She was pale everywhere except for here. Here, she was pink. Pink and perfect and everything he desired. He leaned in, tracing the edge of her puckered nipple with his tongue before sucking her deep into his mouth.

"So sweet," he said, his voice rough and unrecognizable to his own ears. "Better than honey."

She shivered beneath him and he recognized his pleasure coursing through her body. He was learning to read her. Learning to understand what made her moan, what brought her close to the edge. Had learned how to tease her. How to hold her on the brink of climax without giving it to her completely.

He had never kept a lover for this length of time before. Always, he was finished with them after a couple of nights. A couple of weeks was unheard of. There was something…intoxicating about it. Something singular. To know one particular woman's body in such an intimate fashion. Of course, he was well-versed with the female body, but that was different. This was…

Well, this was Elle.

He imagined it would never be the same with another woman, no matter how long he was with her. Elle was a fiery, living fantasy come to life, everything he had ever imagined she might be and more.

It was a damn shame. He wished she was a disappointment. Wished that she was something he could despise. Wished that she could have done something, anything to confirm that he was right to carry out this revenge plot, and use her as he'd planned.

He wished he had left her as the brittle, buttoned-up woman she had seemed in his mind only a couple of weeks ago.

But now he knew her. Knew her body. Knew her soul.

That's ridiculous. You cannot know someone's soul. You haven't one of your own.

He pulled her close, taking hold of the tie on her swimsuit bottoms and tugging the thread roughly, then the other side, letting it fall to the ground. Trying to break the spell that she had cast over him with this bright, insubstantial piece of fabric. It was insane. And yet it was so...

He had advanced no further with her than where he had been nine years ago. He was still a slave to his desires. And now he was old enough to know that going out and getting any redhead at any bar would not suffice.

Now that he had had Elle, he knew that there was no substitute. Ever. There had never been another woman like her, and there never would be again.

He dropped to his knees in front of her, suddenly overwhelmed with his desire. He buried his face between her thighs, tasting her, deep and long, relishing the flavor of her desire as it spread over his tongue. He was insatiable for her. Desperate for her. He pushed one finger deep inside her slick channel, then another, loving the way that she bucked against his hand, the needy cries for pleasure that escaped her lips.

She was desperate. Like he was. She was in this with

him. He needed it proven. Needed to know for sure. He felt like he was losing his mind. He did not know himself now. Never in all his life had a woman made him shake. Never in all his life had a woman owned him in such a way. Never had a woman successfully erased visions of any other.

But she had.

He gripped her hips, holding her tightly against his mouth as he continued to pleasure her, until she shook just as violently as he did. Until she was on the verge. Until she was whimpering, crying out for release. Begging for it.

He loosened his hold on her, sliding the flat of his tongue over her as he rose upward, tracing a line to her belly button, up farther, until he was standing. Until he could capture her mouth with his. He pulled her up against him, let her feel the hard, insistent thrust of his arousal against her stomach. Kissed until he was dizzy. Until she was pleading with him to take her.

He rocked his hips against her, relishing the raw sounds she made, the feeling of her fingernails digging into his skin. It was always like this with her. Desire tinged with violence.

And he loved it.

He backed her up against the bed, and they fell onto it. He positioned himself between her thighs, pressing the head of himself to her slick entrance. He pushed into her easily, her arousal easing the way. She was so hot, so tight. She was made just for him.

As he seated himself fully inside her he had the strongest sensation that he was home. That he was complete for the first time in years.

A deep, strong emotion tugged at his chest, a sense of déjà vu that he didn't want to place. This was new and familiar all at the same time. And he rejected it. Didn't want it. But as his arousal built, as she flexed her hips beneath him, meeting his every thrust, he found he could not hold on to his control and keep the emotions at bay.

She wrapped her legs around his hips, and as she gave herself up to her own release, as his own climax crashed over him like a wave, those feelings crashed through him, as well.

And as he was tossed violently in the surf, he could think of one thing. Elle. That she was the port in the storm. That she was the constant. The North Star by which he had been guided for years. A star he had turned away from.

The realization left him feeling like his chest was full of broken glass. As though he had been wounded, invaded by sharp, shattered splinters he could never hope to remove.

He looked down at Elle, at her lips, flushed with desire, swollen from his kisses, her eyes, slumberous, satisfied. Looking at him as though he held answers.

He had no answers. At this moment, he had nothing but questions.

"Stay with me. Tonight," she said, "could you stay with me?"

And as terror tore at him like a rabid dog, he could do nothing but nod and pull her into his arms. But it did nothing to stop the hemorrhaging in his chest. Did nothing to stem the flow of pure, unmitigated fear pounding through him.

But Elle had asked him to stay. And so he did.

CHAPTER EIGHT

WHEN APOLLO WOKE, it was starting to turn gray outside. And Elle was curled up around him like a cat. He had no doubt, even for a moment, who he was lying in bed with. Who he had fallen asleep with.

He had never been close enough with a woman to even contemplate letting his guard down enough to fall asleep with her. In the past, the moment he finished making love with a woman, he left. There was no reason to linger. Sex, in his experience, could be perfectly impersonal. Sleeping with someone had seemed an intimacy he did not wish to contend with.

But he had fallen asleep with Elle, after she had asked him to stay. He had not imagined he would sleep. But it seemed natural. To hold her in his arms while they both drifted off. Bathing in the afterglow of the pleasure they had shared.

Suddenly, panic overtook him. He had a plan. A plan to make the St. James family pay for the sins they had committed against his family. To avenge the death of his father. The loss of his family fortune. The strange relationship Apollo's mother had been forced into by David St. James.

And every indignity he had suffered. Every moment he had been made to feel like he had not earned his position at the prestigious boarding school he went to. Every time he had to defend his placement in the boardroom because he had come from such humble beginnings.

She was weakening that plan. She was weakening his determination. And he could not let that stand.

He extricated himself from her hold, rolling out of bed. He forked his fingers through his hair, looking around, before remembering he had no clothes in her room. He wrenched open the door, walking down the hall completely naked. All of the staff would have gone home. Anyway, they knew better than to stare too long if they saw something shocking in his home.

Instead of going to his bedroom, he went into his office, taking a bottle of whiskey from the shelf to the left of his desk. He poured a healthy amount, and took a fortifying drink. Elle drove him to drink. This was the second time he'd turned to alcohol to deal with the effects she had on him.

Most women didn't affect him at all.

He had been determined to keep her with him until the attraction between them burned out, but he could see that something else was heating up between them, something he had no hope of burning out half so quickly.

Rage took him over. He didn't want to send her away. He could imagine it, telling her to leave. Never touching her again. Never spending another night with her. Anger overtook him, completely, dictating his next action. He took the half-full glass of whiskey and hurled it at the wall, watching the glass shatter, feeling no remorse at all.

The fact that the very thought of her leaving made him feel so helpless, so enraged was only more evidence that he had to send her away.

If he was going to take his revenge, he would have to take it now.

* * *

They had forgotten to tint the windows. That was Elle's first thought when she woke up the next morning. Her second thought was that she was alone. True to his word, Apollo had not spent the night with her. She shouldn't be surprised, but after she had confessed to him that he was her only lover, she supposed she had expected... something.

She supposed that she was foolish.

For wishing that things could be different. For wishing that something had changed between them. She didn't know what.

She sat up, clutching the blankets to her chest. And suddenly, Apollo came bursting through the door. "Good morning," he said, his mouth set into a grim line.

"Good morning," she said.

During all of the time she'd spent here, he had never come into her room unannounced. He had never come in unless it was to make love. He did not look like he had... that on his mind. Not in the least. He looked... He looked like he had come in with demons on his heels.

"I trust you slept well," he said.

"Yes," she said, a strange, uneasy feeling settling in the center of her chest. She didn't know why. She only knew that something wasn't right.

"I think it is time you left," he said, his words cold.

"But we... I don't understand," she said. "Yesterday we..."

"That was yesterday. And this is today."

She thought back to last night, to what had transpired between them. Had she done something wrong? Had he not liked her wearing the bikini and reminding him of that day? No. Yesterday he had enjoyed it. She knew he had.

"I'm not ready to leave," she said. "We agreed we needed to burn this out and I don't think it's burned out."

"A difference of opinion," he said, his tone hard. "For me, it is over."

"Apollo…"

"Also, effective immediately you have been terminated from your position as CEO of Matte."

"I… What?" She couldn't make sense of his words. She was naked, in bed, after having just spent the night making love with him, and he was firing her.

Two weeks. Two weeks she had spent with this man. In his arms. Kissing him, sharing her body with him… sharing everything.

"You heard me," he continued. His tone was flat. His eyes were flat. He was like a stranger. Only yesterday she had felt that she'd known him more intimately, more deeply than any other person on earth. And now she doubted it. She truly did. "I grow tired of the charade, Elle. Truth be told, I was planning on drawing this out longer. I was anticipating feeling a great sense of pleasure when I let you know that I was simply using you to hurt your father. I planned to set you up as the face of the company, to bring you into greater prominence so that when I made it very clear that I had taken all of your father's assets and left him ruined, the world would know exactly who he was, exactly what that meant. But frankly, I find it's just too tiring. So, I will have to be content in my revenge all on my own."

Her head was spinning. Revenge? She had been under no illusions that there was any affection between Apollo and her, but if anyone should want revenge, it was her. "You… You used me."

"Did you really think that I wanted you?"

She felt like he had driven a spike through her chest.

The cold, black words matching his cold, black eyes, making it impossible to pretend she had misheard. "Of course I did. As far as I know men can't fake…" She gestured toward the front of his pants. "They have to at least be attracted to a woman."

"It isn't just women who can lie back and think of England. What I really wanted, Elle, was to let your father know that I've taken everything from him. What would he think if he knew—?"

"Don't you dare, you bastard."

"Then I would have his company, and his daughter."

"You don't have me," she said, her throat tightening. "Two weeks, Apollo. Two weeks I gave you… I did…" She swallowed hard, panic taking over, tears threatening to fall. "I held nothing back from you! I trusted you with my body."

"A bad decision. I am untrustworthy. I have been from the beginning. You were convenient, darling, but let's be honest. Hardly more than a diversion, and one I cannot afford anymore."

"How can you say that?"

"It's true. Elle, be realistic. What could I possibly want with a near-virgin who's so cold she practically leaves icicles on my lips after a kiss?"

His words struck her like a physical blow. None of this made sense. She couldn't process it. But somewhere, in the middle of all the pain, all the anguish flooding through her like an unchecked tide, she found rage. The same rage that had propelled her into his arms in the first place.

And she clung it to it with everything she had. "How dare you?" she hissed, low and hard. "My father did everything for you. He paid for your education. He loved you—"

"No," he said. "He never loved me. He wanted to possess my mother, at any cost. And he did so. His very own Biblical fantasy where she was his Bathsheba and he sent her husband out to die."

"What?"

"Yes. My family was not always impoverished. Your father and mine were business partners, Elle. But they both fell for the same woman. My mother. She preferred my father. Your father bided his time, waited until he saw the opportunity, and then he used his sway with the board to vote my father out of the company. My father was ruined. Ultimately, he killed himself. My mother held out against your father's pleas for him to join her in the US. As his mistress. He was of course married to your mother then."

"I…"

"My mother agreed when I was eight, and we were starving. He established us in a home near his, and he came to visit often. From what I discovered later, he paid your mother off, then waited an appropriate amount of time before bringing my mother to the estate to be his wife."

"No… My father wouldn't… He didn't…"

"He did. He's a manipulative bastard who sees us all as nothing more than pawns. His actions caused my father to kill himself, it ruined my family. But I started to look into the history of my family. And when I found out why my father killed himself…why he was ruined…it all became clear." He paused. "It was your mother who contacted me."

Elle's mother who had long since abandoned the family. Whom Elle hadn't seen in fifteen years. "My mother?"

"Yes. She had seen me rising in business circles and

she…she found me one night at a bar. I didn't know who she was. Just another blonde who was after a night, I thought. But unlike most women, she didn't want sex. She wanted to talk. She wanted to tell me just what your father was."

"She came and found you? After all these years, not speaking to me for any of them, she came and found *you*? Are you that much more compelling to both of my parents?"

"In her case, I think she was compelled by revenge."

"Did she even ask about me?" Elle asked, despising the small sound of her own voice.

He said nothing, and it was his silence that spoke loudest. Of course she hadn't. She hadn't contacted her in years, why would she be concerned now? "I can't… I don't know what to think. I don't know how to process this."

His top lip curled. "Well, you will have plenty of time to process it while you stand in line filing paperwork to collect unemployment."

"Apollo… You can't do this."

His expression was granite. "I am doing this. It was my plan all along, and I am keeping to it. I am simply shortening the timeline."

Her stomach tightened, her entire body seizing up. She thought she was breaking apart from the inside out.

She had believed in him. Believed that he was the first person to see her for who she was. To want her for herself.

That was the worst betrayal of all. The fact that he'd used her. Not even because he hated her, not even because he wanted revenge on her, but because he wanted it on her *father*. Yet again, she was nothing. Nothing more than the most convenient chess piece on the board.

"Get out," she said, shaking now, trembling inside and out.

"It is my house."

"And it is my room. Leave me with what little dignity I have left." He turned away from her, heading toward the door. "I can't believe you. All the things you let me say. All the things you let me do. The bikini. As if I was... As if I mattered. But I never did. You're not any better than my father. Even if what you say is true, every word of it, you haven't risen above anything."

He turned back to her, his expression bleak. "I never wanted to rise above. I only ever wanted to drag you all into hell with me."

And with that, he walked out of the room, leaving her there, desolate and broken and certain she would never be whole again.

CHAPTER NINE

"IF YOU DON'T mind me saying, Mr. Savas, you've been impossible the past few weeks."

"I know *you* don't mind saying it, Alethea," he said, his tone hard as he looked at his computer screen, ignoring his assistant.

"It's true," she said, turning on her heel and walking out of the office. Apollo didn't look up until the door had been shut firmly behind her.

Damned woman. She was always speaking the truth. He should fire her and hire someone stupid, beautiful and biddable.

When he thought the word *beautiful*, only one face came to mind. Of course, that woman was neither stupid, nor biddable. And she was persistently in his head.

Particularly in his dreams. He had woken up hard and reaching for her and she wasn't there. Because he'd sent her away.

It had seemed necessary at the time. Like he needed to put distance between them. But the longer he spent without her, the more he questioned that decision.

After all, his issue had been his loss of control, but sending her away wasn't any more controlled.

He had removed temptation from his path, but he had

not successfully destroyed his lust for her. Because of that, he was suffering now.

There was no reason to do so, of course. She had nothing to do, nowhere to go. No job. He could have her back. Make her his.

The memory of her—the warm weight of her, her sweet scent, the way she sighed and said his name—haunted him. His days, his nights.

He was like an addict in desperate need of a fix. His hands shaking, sweat breaking out over his skin at the thought of tasting her lips. Feeling her softness beneath his palms.

She was his own personal designer drug. One taste had only sent him headlong into an addiction he couldn't shake.

So maybe that was the problem. Cutting himself off completely would never work. It would only leave him wondering what it would be like to have her one last time. To lose himself inside her. To feel her delicate fingertips skimming over his back.

Just the thought sent a rush of need through him, so hot, so swift it nearly sent him down to his knees.

He had never felt like this before. Had never felt the need to keep and possess quite so fiercely.

As her father felt for your mother?

No. This was different. But one thing he knew: he had spent too many years denying this desire. He would not continue on.

He had been forced into denial, into poverty as a boy because of her father.

He would not subject himself to denial of his needs again.

He would not go one more night without her in his bed.

* * *

Elle was certain she was dying. It had been four weeks since she had left Greece. Four weeks since she had left Apollo, jobless, broken and humiliated. At least none of it had made it out into the public.

All anyone knew was that she had been replaced in her position at Matte. No one knew about her relationship with Apollo, and that was about the only thing saving her from melting into a puddle and sliding down the nearest drain, disappearing forever.

As upset as her father was about the entire situation, at least he didn't blame her. Or, maybe she didn't care. She had no idea how she felt. In only a month her entire life had been completely upended. She was avoiding her father. Avoiding dealing with that situation entirely.

Everything Apollo had said, all of the things he had told her that her father was guilty of, had settled down deep inside of her, and created just enough doubt about… everything that she wasn't sure she could deal with right now.

And then, purely selfishly, there was the issue of her firing.

She stood up, the floor pitching beneath her as she rose from the couch for the first time in hours. Being unemployed was bad for her wardrobe choices. She had been wearing sweats for three days, because there was no one there to see her anyway. Yesterday she'd worn flannels with small foxes on them. Today, her pants had owls.

"Very sexy," she said, crossing the length of the apartment and heading toward her fridge. She opened it up, immediately swamped by the smell coming from the inside. She wrinkled her nose. Something did not smell right. But it wasn't like she kept that much food in the fridge.

She dry heaved, and slammed the door shut. She'd forced herself to eat when she'd first woken up, but nothing tasted like…anything. A broken heart did that to you, apparently. But any semblance of an appetite she might have was gone now.

She felt like she had licked the inside of the tennis shoe. Okay, that thought made her stomach feel even worse.

She heard a knock on her door, and she nearly jumped out of her skin. People didn't just gain admittance to the building, so it had to be someone who already lived here. Though, her neighbors didn't speak to her, so she had no idea who it was or what it could be about.

Taking a deep breath, she crossed the apartment and undid the dead bolt and the chain, jerking it open just as she realized she should have looked through the peephole first.

But it was too late. The door was open, and standing there was her worst nightmare.

Suddenly, the vague sense of nausea intensified and she ran from the room, losing her breakfast violently in the bathroom.

"Elle?" Apollo's voice was coming from behind her.

"Stay away," she said, shakily getting to her feet. "I'm…horrifying."

"You're sick," he said, his tone vaguely accusatory.

"I…wasn't." Except she had been—though not this sick—but off her game for the past few days.

"What are you doing here, anyway?" She wandered over to the sink and splashed cold water on her face. "Who buzzed you in?"

"Some young woman who lives down the hall. Nose ring. Pink hair. She thought I looked trustworthy."

Elle laughed. Bitter, hollow. "She thought you looked like you belonged in her bed. I would give her advanced warning, but I imagine she wouldn't really care either way."

"Sadly for her. I'm not on the market."

"Okay. If you aren't here to hook up with my down-the-hall neighbor, why are you here?"

"Would you believe that I came to check on you?"

"No."

"I want you back."

"No," she said, her tone incredulous. "You can't have me back. You were awful to me. You fired me."

"And now you don't have a job. I thought you might be interested in pursuing some sort of arrangement."

She laughed, flinging her arms wide. "And here I am, vomiting as you ask me to come be your mistress. Really, there are probably more romantic settings than the bathroom."

"You need money. You certainly need a way to occupy your time."

"You're despicable."

She swept past him, trying to hold her head high. Difficult to do when the man who had made love to you then humiliated you had just seen you puke.

"Maybe," he said, lingering in the door frame, bracing his hands against it. "But it doesn't change the facts."

"Oh," she said, the world tilting slightly. "I need to lie down."

He frowned. "How long have you been feeling sick?"

"I told you, I only just… That, in the bathroom."

"You've been otherwise feeling well?"

"Not really. But then, you humiliated me and fired

me. So I don't know how well you could possibly expect me to feel."

"I'm not talking about your emotions, I'm talking about physically."

"No. I have not been feeling very well. But your emotions inform things like that."

"Have you gotten your period?"

Her mouth dropped open. "What kind of question is that?"

"The only question that matters to me right now."

Ice shivered down her spine. "I haven't," she said. "But that doesn't… It doesn't mean anything."

"You're here vomiting and looking pale, you haven't had your period in the past month and you don't think that means anything."

"We…"

"Were not very careful."

No, they hadn't been. They hadn't used a condom in the elevator, and again during that last time at his home. So really… She hadn't had a period since the elevator. "No, I guess we weren't."

"And it didn't occur to you until just now that you might be pregnant?"

"No," she said, her hand flying to her mouth, her eyes wide. "No. I'm not… I'm not."

"You have no way of knowing that."

No. She didn't. Because she hadn't taken a test. And, while she had never been particularly regular, that hadn't exactly been a problem because she had been a virgin. Now…it was a bit suspicious.

"I mean, I would prefer to wait a few days…"

He had already pulled out a cell phone. "Yes, Alethea? Find a discreet women's doctor in Manhattan who can see a patient immediately. Text me the information once you have it. When I say immediately, I mean I'm about to get in the car and start driving. They had better be ready to see us."

He hung up, and she could only stare at him. "What are you doing?"

"We are going to answer this question once and for all, *agape*. And make no mistake, if you are carrying my child there is no question that you are coming back to Greece with me. Immediately."

He could do nothing but pace outside the office at the posh, private medical facility he had taken Elle to.

He had found himself back in Manhattan for business reasons, and then he had displayed a characteristic weakness and found himself at Elle's building.

He did not know what manner of witchcraft Elle possessed that she made it impossible for him to forget her. Forget how she made him feel. Whether it was four weeks in the past, or nine years—before he had ever even touched her. She was a woman who lingered in his mind in a way that none before her—or since—ever had.

He wondered now if she had been some sort of bad omen. If the fact that he had never been able to get her out of his mind had been a warning of some kind. If she were truly pregnant with his child, he could not discount that. He had never intended to have children. But the moment the idea that she might be pregnant had entered his mind he had known that he would take possession of his child.

After his own childhood, after the way he had lost his father, he knew he would never subject his own child to such a thing. To a life without the man who was meant to protect him.

He gritted his teeth. His own father's feelings had hardly been his fault. He had been pushed into ruin by

David St. James. The fault would always lie with St. James. Apollo however was standing on his own two feet. No one was pushing him anywhere.

The door opened, and Elle emerged, clutching a few pieces of paper, her face pale. He didn't need her to speak to know what the answer was.

He had never imagined being in this situation. He supposed that any man who was sexually active could potentially face it, but he had always been very careful. So it was never anything he had considered seriously. But he had not been careful with Elle. The theme in their relationship, and the consequences of that, were now coming home to roost.

There was no panic. There was not even any rage, though he had expected it. No, there was nothing but cold, clean determination. He knew exactly what he was going to do. What he would demand.

"I…"

"Yes, I think I can guess."

"I don't know what we're going to do."

"I know exactly what we are going to do."

Her eyes widened. "You do?"

"Yes. You will be coming back to Athens with me. And then, *agape*, you and I are going to marry."

Elle was dimly aware of the fact that she was sitting in Apollo's limo, essentially in a catatonic state. But she had just found out she was pregnant with the baby of a man who despised her and her family, a man who had left her jobless and broken when he had ended their affair.

She had never really thought about being a mother. Her own mother had abandoned her early on and not bothered to keep in touch at all. Her stepmother was a lovely woman, but often silent next to her husband.

And Elle's father was so...imposing. He didn't bend. He didn't show affection. It was like loving a rock.

She had never imagined trying to re-create that parent-child relationship with herself in the parenting hot seat. It seemed...completely unappealing. It also meant she was linked to Apollo. Forever.

As if you weren't before.

She gritted her teeth. She had no idea what to say. No idea what to do next. And as far as she knew she was being shanghaied and sent to Athens again.

That thought sent her into action. "I'm not going to marry you."

He chuckled, a dark, humorless sound. "Then prepare yourself for a custody battle that will drain you of your every resource."

She blinked. "Who said I would fight you for custody?"

The moment she said it, she realized that she would. Not because her parents had been wonderful, not because they had made her long for a parent-child relationship in her own life. But because they had demonstrated in a million small ways how unimportant she was. She would be damned if her own child would walk through life feeling like their mother couldn't be bothered with them.

Just the thought made her stomach clench in agony. Her own little one, believing that she didn't want them. She wanted to apologize to the little life inside her. As though it had somehow sensed her hesitance.

"If you don't feel strongly enough about our child to stand and fight for them, then I would gladly have you step aside."

"I won't," she said, her tone infused with conviction.

The numbness was starting to wear off. And even though she couldn't quite imagine what it would be like to have a child, even though she wasn't sure if she was devastated or happy, she knew that she wouldn't stand aside.

"You just said—"

"Yes, well, I am trying to figure out exactly where I stand. It might surprise you to know this but I didn't exactly fantasize about a life with a picket fence, a husband and children."

"It doesn't surprise me. A woman with as much white in her apartment as you have doesn't seem to be planning ahead for sticky fingers."

"I wasn't. You can be sure of that. But I'm also not one to walk away from my responsibilities. And I don't want any child of mine going through life imagining they aren't wanted."

"Then, marriage it will be."

Her mind was ticking over at a million miles a minute. "I would have a few conditions," she said.

She could not believe she had just said that. She knew that you weren't supposed to negotiate with terrorists or superalpha Greek billionaires who had far too high of an opinion of themselves. So, she didn't know why she was attempting it.

"Conditions, *agape*?" He sounded…angry. But interested.

"Yes. Conditions." Now she had to quickly think of her conditions. "New York is my home. I'm not leaving New York."

"I have a villa in Greece."

"I daresay you have homes all over the world. I know you don't have a permanent residence in New York, but I do."

"Your apartment is the size of a postage stamp."

"It's big enough."

"For you. There is no room for a child. No room for a husband."

She gritted her teeth. "I did not agree to taking a husband. Not yet. I have conditions, but I won't make my final decision until I'm certain that the situation is to my liking."

"I'm not certain you want to challenge my authority. I am a well-respected billionaire, after all, and you are unemployed. The daughter of a businessman on the verge of being washed-up. If your mother hasn't spent all of his payoff money by now, she's certainly close to it. What could you possibly give a child that I can't?"

"Love. Warmth. Human emotion?"

"I'm sure the court will be more impressed with my net worth."

"I don't think so. Everyone agrees that a child needs love above anything else."

"And you feel you are more qualified to give a child parental love that I am?"

She shifted in her seat. "Yes. I do."

"On what grounds? Prior to being unemployed you were a workaholic."

"I was not."

"Did you have a single friend who was not also a co-worker?"

She didn't even have to think about that. She knew the answer to the question. But whether or not they were from work Suki and Christine were real friends. Suki had brought cupcakes after Elle had been fired. *Friendship.*

Though the thought of cupcakes made her stomach turn right now.

"You're a workaholic, too," she said.

"I'm also a man and a billionaire. No one will judge

me for the amount of time I spend working. It is irrelevant. Not so for you."

"The point is, I am the child's mother and I don't think I'm going to have an issue retaining custody."

"I disagree."

"You will have to wait, Apollo," she said, her voice infused with iron, with a strength she wasn't sure she truly felt right now. "I'm not afraid of fighting you in court. To hear you tell it your mother was manipulated into a relationship with my father and now you want to do the same to me? How are you any better?"

"I'm not," he said, his expression bleak, cold. But only for a moment. Then his walls went back up.

"Name your conditions clearly."

"I want to stay in New York. I wish to have the child here. I wish to raise him here."

"The child will be Greek. He should be exposed to his homeland."

"Exposure is fine. But I want him raised here. I want to stay here. Because that leads me to my next requirement. I want my job back."

"The new CEO has only been there for a month. If I let him go I will seem capricious."

"There is a cost to everything. And that is the cost to having me without muss or fuss. Do you accept, or not?"

She wasn't certain if she wanted him to say yes, or if she wanted him to refuse. She wasn't sure what she wanted at all.

"I accept."

A strange mixture of relief and terror washed through her. "Excellent."

He pulled out his phone again. "Alethea," he said. "I require some real estate. A penthouse, Manhattan. Something large, but secure. No rooftop balconies or anything like that. Or, if there are balconies, they need to be se-cure. Childproof." He hung up.

"Is your assistant finding you a house?"

"No, *agape*," he said, smiling a smile that was not friendly at all. "My assistant is going to find us a home. Now do you agree to marry me?"

Elle took a deep breath and met that coal-black gaze. "If I find the conditions are met to my satisfaction. And if I feel you won't spend my whole life making me mis-erable. You said I was your revenge, Apollo. Until you see me as a woman—a whole woman, not your stepsis-ter who you harbor rage against, not an instrument of vengeance to use against my father—you will not have me. Not in your life, not as your wife. That's a promise."

CHAPTER TEN

ALETHEA WAS NOTHING if not efficient, and by that afternoon he and Elle were standing in an empty penthouse at the top of the building in Midtown. It was spacious, though hardly the sun-drenched villa he chose to call home in Greece. But it would do.

"Do you find this satisfactory?"

"I have a… I have a house," she said.

"Oh, I have already taken care of listing it for you. Unless you wish to keep it as some sort of workspace, I figured it would be best to sell it."

"You're selling my house?"

"My men have been over there packing your things."

She whirled around, her hands clenched into fists. "Apollo! I can't believe you would do something like that."

He turned to her, arching a dark brow. "Really. You can't believe I would do something like that? And here I thought it was in keeping with my character."

She pressed her fists up against her eyes, as though she was trying to use them to hold back her rage. "Everything is changing too quickly."

"Things have been changing quickly for the past two months. First, we had sex. Then you went to Greece. Then we had more sex. You lost your job. Now you're having a baby and we're working at integrating our lives. It's a fast-moving train, life is."

In truth, his life had been stagnant for quite a few years. Yes, he had more money than he could possibly spend in a lifetime. His business had continued to grow. He had fixated on his revenge plan against the St. James family. But beyond that, nothing had moved significantly in years. His life was an endless array of beautiful women, meaningless events that required him to put on a suit and smile politely at those in attendance. This was...

This was the first time in a long time he had something new.

It wasn't the revenge he had planned when he'd come back to New York, but it was...interesting. He imagined Elle would take exception to him calling her accidental pregnancy interesting.

"Fine. It's very you. But you can't just come into my life and completely reorder it."

"Why not? You have done it to me."

She looked stunned for a moment. "Have I?"

"You are going to make me a father. If that is not upending my life, I don't know what is."

"I suppose it depends on how involved you intend to be."

He knew nothing about how to be a good father. He could scarcely remember his own. When the other man had been alive he had all but lived at the corporate headquarters for the business he shared with David St. James. And then, after that, after the disgrace, he had sunk into drugs and alcohol. Affairs. Only a few years later he was dead.

As far as David went...the man had been an attentive stepfather. He had been... Well, none of it mattered now. Because of what he had revealed himself to be.

"I am a busy man. A wealthy man. I plan to keep my involvement somewhat limited," he said.

"Then, I suppose your personal life doesn't have to change much. Oh," she said, her green gaze turning sharp. "Except you are required to remain faithful to me."

Her words hit him low and hard in the stomach. Punched the wound he had just been examining. He could not imagine wanting a woman other than Elle. He had not taken anyone else to his bed in the month since they had parted. Unusual for him.

In fact, from the moment he had taken over her father's company, from the moment he had first taken over the magazine and brought her back into his life on a semi-regular basis, he had not been with another woman. Because the moment Elle St. James had come back into his life his body had reignited its obsession for her. Still, he did not wish for her to know that. He did not want her issuing more edicts.

He had agreed to New York, because that was simple. He had agreed to giving her the position at Matte back because it was also simple. And quite apart from that, the fact that he was providing David St. James with his first grandchild was a whole new, delicious sort of revenge.

He no longer needed to throw her out of the company. No longer required to destroy St. James in that way. He had the man's daughter. She was having his baby. She would be his wife, Apollo was confident in that.

Yes, there was a great deal he could do with that. He was certain.

"I have no experience with fidelity," he said. "I will make no promises on that score."

"Then you will enjoy the single life. If you touch another woman, you certainly won't be touching me."

"I highly doubt that."

He and Elle could scarcely be in the same room together without tearing each other's clothes off. Today was an exception, brought about by the shock of her discovering she was pregnant and by the need to see to the logistics created by that circumstance. But he knew that very soon he would have her on her back begging for his possession.

Or she will have you on your back begging for hers.

He refused to consider that. Refused to think of things that way. She was a slave to the pleasure that ignited between them every time they touched, just as he was. He was not at a disadvantage. He was not alone in it.

"The perk of staying single is that I will be free to pursue other lovers," she said, shaking her head, her coppery mane shimmering in the sunlight filtering through the large windows that overlooked Central Park.

"I don't believe that," he said, rage a hot, living thing in his stomach. The thought of another man touching Elle was anathema. But she was bluffing, and he would call her on that.

"Why is that? I may have been a virgin before you and I met, Apollo, but now that you have shown me just how enjoyable sex can be I don't think you can possibly ask me to forgo the pleasure."

"I damn well can."

She laughed. "Careful. Your desperation is showing. You wouldn't want me to understand where my real power is in all of this."

She hit too close to the bone there, cut him far too deeply.

And suddenly, he did not care that today had been an emotional one for her. He did not care that she was in a fragile state. Only than only a couple of hours ago she had been sick in front of him, while wearing sweatpants. He always wanted Elle. Always. There was never a time when he didn't crave her touch. And this was no exception.

He crossed the vacant expanse of the living area, wrapping his arm around her waist and tugging her up against him, cupping her chin with his thumb and forefinger. "Do not push me, Elle. You will not like the result."

"Do not push *me*, Apollo."

"We push each other, *agape*, that's the honest truth. And look at where it has gotten us."

"Yes. I daresay it is not the most pleasant situation."

"I could make it much more pleasant if you weren't so stubborn."

She glared at him. "The same goes for you."

"You start again at Matte tomorrow. I will give your replacement a generous severance."

He released his hold on her.

"Excellent," she said, smoothing her clothing, her voice making it sound like she thought all of this was anything but excellent.

"I have arranged for all of our things to be moved into the penthouse by tonight."

She laughed. "That isn't possible."

He lifted his shoulder. "It is possible when you pay with cash."

She shook her head. "That's the problem with you, Apollo, you have never been denied anything that you wanted."

"I don't know, Elle, I felt fairly denied of my father after he put a bullet in his brain. And why did he do that? Oh, yes. Because his dear friend and business partner betrayed him. Yes, I know a little bit about deprivation. I refuse to apologize for enjoying luxury now."

She blinked. "I'm sorry. I didn't mean…"

He waved a hand. "I am not so sensitive. Anyway, this is par for the course between us, yes? We must tear strips off each other's hides. Because if we do not, we will tear each other's clothes off instead."

She sniffed. "Maybe once. But not anymore."

"You may cling to that illusion all you want. Either way, your things will be here by this evening. How you choose to spend your time between now and then is up to you."

The next day, when Elle walked into the fully furnished penthouse she felt dazed. Her life was changing so quickly. They were going to be sharing a space while he was in New York. Living together. And he wanted to marry her.

It made her stomach tight. Made her feel dizzy.

The terrifying thing was there was some small, delusional piece of her that felt…excited. As though this were some kind of fairy tale. As though the two of them were embarking on a real relationship. Possibly, a real marriage. As though he wanted her, because she was Elle, because of the heat and fire between them, not because she was carrying his baby.

He came back. He came back before he knew you were pregnant.

She held that close. Turned it over and examined it as though it was some kind of rare treasure that she wanted to keep shielded from the world. That she never wanted to look away from. He had returned to her before he found out about the baby. She didn't know what that meant. Yes, he had said he wanted her to return as his mistress. But she knew full well that a man like Apollo was more than capable of getting any woman he desired. He didn't need her. But he had still come for her.

And the moment he had found out about the baby he had taken charge, taken everything into hand and done everything he could to make their arrangement permanent.

It was perhaps foolish to assign any meaning to that, but she couldn't help it.

At the bottom of it all, at the end of everything, she just wanted someone who wanted to be with her. Maybe that was a sad admission. But she had been lonely for so long. For all of her life. And the way that Apollo looked at her, the way that he commanded her body, so fierce and intense, at the exclusion of all else, made her hopeful that there was more to his attentions than he was willing to admit.

Of course, he would not promise to be faithful to her.

She blinked, swallowing hard, continuing to examine the modern layout of the penthouse. "Which room will be mine?"

"Any one that you choose," he said. "Though the master bedroom already has your things in it."

"Not yours?"

He lifted his shoulder. "I have several other residences. I may not always be here as frequently as you are. My headquarters will remain in Greece. That means I will only spend a small amount of time here."

The idea of him being with other women flooded her mind again. Of course. He wasn't actually planning on living with her. Not really. Not all the time. He was taking possession of her, but he was holding her at arm's length. It shouldn't surprise her. But it did hurt.

And it did nothing to remove the traitorous beacon of hope that still burned down in the pit of her stomach. She should harbor no hope where he was concerned, and still that small part of her whispered: *But he came back before he knew about the baby.*

She wasn't going to let him see her hope.

"That's fine. It will be good for the child, I think, to have us in the same house sometimes. At least there is space. I think I might go lie down," she said, heading toward the stairs that led to the upper level of the penthouse and the bedrooms.

"You're welcome to. But we have a dinner reservation in four hours. I expect you to be ready by then."

She gritted her teeth. "Is this going to be nothing more than a series of edicts?"

"You keep challenging them, I keep trying."

"Well, thankfully a meal is not a marriage."

She continued on up the stairs. Then she walked down the hall and pushed open the door to her new bedroom. In her new house. Suddenly, her knees felt like they were going to buckle. Everything was so overwhelming. The decisions she suddenly had to make. She moved quickly to the bed and threw herself down on the soft surface. And then she did the thing she allowed so very rarely. She buried her face in the pillow and wept.

Elle was always beautiful. That was part of the problem with her. No matter that she was forbidden, either because she was his stepsister or the daughter of his enemy, she was too beautiful. But tonight, in a short cream lace dress, her skin looking as waxen as a doll's, her red hair falling softly around her shoulders, she was like a particularly terrified angel. Otherworldly. Ethereal.

And all he could think of was that he wanted to drag her into the pit with him. Make her fall, as he had done.

He had not lied when he had told her that all he had ever wanted was to bring her down to his level. To somehow make it acceptable for a man like him to touch a woman like her.

What does it matter what is acceptable?

He didn't even know what was acceptable anymore. So the question, he supposed, was moot.

He had not told her what the aim of the dinner was. She would be angry at him, but he could not see her resisting once she saw the ring.

He had gone to a jewelry store today and chosen the ring for her himself. A large square-cut champagne diamond that seemed to capture her particular brand of unique elegance better than a standard sort of engagement ring.

He had also chosen one of the most up-and-coming restaurants in Manhattan to perform the deed. Because there was guaranteed to be paparazzi lurking, even if they were hiding in the hedgerows, so to speak. And, beyond that, there would be people there with cameras ready to take pictures and post what they had seen to the internet. Getting the word out had never been so easy, and since discretion was the furthest thing from his mind, it suited him.

He took her hand, running his thumb over the smooth, silken skin. Some unknown, possessive, caveman part of him relished what was about to happen. The fact that soon he would put his ring on her finger, and the world would know that she belonged to him. He gloried in that. The fact that there would be a sign of his ownership of her.

That made him think of the baby. Of the fact that she would soon grow round with it, yet more evidence of the fact that he had bound her to him, irrevocably, intensely.

He did not know who he was just now. But then, with Elle, he never did.

She looked down at his hand as though it was a potentially dangerous snake. "I don't think you brought me here simply to treat me to a nice meal. Though, it was nice."

"And we have not yet gotten to dessert."

She drew her hand back slowly. "No, we haven't. And you have been perfectly pleasant bordering on solicitous through the entire meal. And so, I need to know what's happening."

"I had planned to wait until you were finished with your cake, *agape*, but if you are feeling impatient then I am more than happy to reveal the reason why I have brought you out tonight."

He reached into the interior pocket of his suit jacket and produced a small velvet box. Though he had not imagined it possible, more color drained from Elle's face. "Is that…"

He shifted from his position in the chair, moving forward, dropping down to one knee in front of where Elle sat. This was yet another thing he had not imagined doing in all of his life. Lowering himself like this. Getting on his knees before a woman. But if the charade was going to work then he had to commit to it. There could be no doing this halfway.

"Elle St. James, I would be very honored if you would accept the offer to become my wife."

He could feel the eyes of all the diners in the restaurant on them, could sense that everyone was watching. And then he heard the sound of shutters. And he knew that it was being documented, just as he had planned. Knew that it would be a headline in the business pages by tomorrow.

"I—I told you I couldn't answer this now," she said, her tone hushed.

If Elle hesitated, she would potentially cause trouble

for him. Perhaps, in his arrogance, he had overplayed his hand.

"I wish for you to become my wife," he said. "You are the only woman I have ever imagined spending my life with. Please, do me the honor of saying yes."

It was the truth, even if it was a misleading truth. In all honesty, he had never imagined taking another woman as his wife. But then, he had not begun thinking about taking Elle for a wife until this morning. So, he supposed there was room for interpretation with those words. But they were not a lie.

Yet her expression remained set.

"Would you like to see the ring?" he asked. If he was not enough enticement then perhaps the jewelry would be.

He opened the lid on the jewelry box, revealing his carefully chosen selection.

She looked at it, her face frozen. Unreadable. She lifted her hand, as though she was going to reach out and touch it, before drawing her hand back quickly, as if the ring was a snake that might bite her.

"No," she said.

"No?" he asked. He was on his knees, on the damn floor in the damn restaurant, and she had refused him.

He felt...at a loss, and that was completely foreign to him. And along with that hollow feeling came...pain. Deep. Stabbing.

She stood suddenly, stumbling around him. "I don't think I want dessert," she said, her voice strangled.

"Are you certain?"

"Yes. I told you I wasn't sure what I wanted and you—" she looked around the room "—you did your best to make this public so that I couldn't say no. You don't get to behave this way, Apollo. I'm not your pawn. I'm not anyone's pawn."

"We will speak more in the car," he said. "There is no point in discussing it here."

"Of course not," she said, "we would not wish for me to make a scene."

He did not have to worry about the check, as the restaurant already had his details, so he took hold of Elle's hand, and the two of them made their way from the restaurant, still with the watchful eyes of the other patrons on them. A quick push of a button on his phone, and his car was brought around to the front. He opened the door for her, then slid inside, and the two of them remained silent until his driver pulled away from the curb. After issuing instructions to take them home he raised the partition between the front seat and the back, shrouding them in privacy.

"Is everything a game to you?" she asked, once they were alone, her expression fierce.

"It is not a game," he said, his voice hard. "It is a strategy. I have spent the past several years planning my revenge against your family. I was finished with it. But now, here you are, and you are pregnant with my baby. I want what I want, Elle, and I intend on getting it."

"So what? You thought you could shock me into saying yes?"

"I thought the ring might do it." It had never occurred to him it might not. Had never truly occurred to him she might refuse.

"If I wanted a ring, I would buy my own. One that did not come with a husband attached."

"Marriage makes sense," he insisted.

"I don't care about sense!" she shouted, her voice filling up the space in the car. "None of this, not ever, not from the first time we touched, was ever about sense."

"Then why pretend it matters now? Why resist me when we both know you're going to give in?"

"Because you would say things like that. Because you think me giving in to you is an inevitability. Because you do not listen, damn you!"

"You're still behaving like you have a choice here," he said, hardening his voice.

"I'm a fool. I keep expecting to discover you feel *something* for me. Anything."

Her words were raw, honest, not the shotgun shells filled with anger her statements typically were. There was a vulnerability here. An honesty he had not anticipated. They scraped at him, tore strips from his hide.

"Of course I feel something for you," he said. "I want you." The words were much more raw, much more shattered than he wanted them to be. But he was rapidly losing control. Of this moment. Of himself.

It was always so with Elle. Always.

She shook her head. "That is not the same thing."

"And yet, it is all I have."

"Because you hate my family so much?"

"Touching you was a betrayal of my father. Of my mother. I had thought to take the thing between us and twist it into something I can use."

"You're that angry?"

"Everything that I built my life around was a lie," he said, his words escaping with a force that shocked him. "I thought your father simply cared about me. Instead, it was all a part of his twisted obsession with my mother. He allowed me to care for him, acted as though he cared for me, while the whole time he knew…he knew he was the reason my father killed himself. So you tell me, Elle, in my position would you not also crave revenge?"

"It solves nothing," she said. "You had your revenge in

hand. You had it for four weeks, you thought it was finished. You had ousted me from my position as CEO. You were done with me. Done with my family, and yet still you were back at my door. So tell me, Apollo, what has revenge solved for you? What has it fixed? Your father is still gone. And you still want me. You are in fact begging me to be your wife. Where is your power in revenge?"

He could not deny it, though he wished to. Though he wished he could tell her that he had been using her all along. He had shown his hand when he had returned to her apartment. When he had asked for her to be his mistress.

And it was not only to her he had shown his hand, but to himself.

"I want you," he said. "Quite apart from any plans for revenge."

"You think that would make a marriage work?"

"It would work because we would make it work. We are attracted to each other, is that not enough?"

"I don't know. I never gave serious thought to marriage. I don't know what I want out of one." She blinked. "Except I would like more than screaming at my husband. I would like more than wondering if he is away having an affair. I would like to be chosen. Just once. Not because of someone else. You know, I'm only the CEO of Matte because it was my father's last attempt to keep hold of his empire. And you… What you really want is to make me your wife so you can lord it over my father."

"I know you don't put stock in my desire for you, because it isn't emotional. I am not capable of the kind of emotion you are talking about. But I will tell you that had I been able to want any other woman, had I had dominion over my desire for you—I never would have given in."

"I'm supposed to rejoice because you didn't *want* to want me?"

"Yes," he said, simply.

"You truly are arrogant. And you don't understand women very well."

He chuckled. "I understand parts of a woman."

"I can't deny that. But I can also tell you that it leaves you cold after, no matter how hot you burn in the moment."

CHAPTER ELEVEN

ELLE FELT DEFLATED by the time they arrived back at the penthouse. She said nothing to him as they went inside, as she walked back to her bedroom and stripped off her jewelry. How had she ever thought she could handle this man? This man who was so twisted by his desire to injure her family that he was willing to consider anyone who stood in his way as collateral damage.

If he acted like a human man, with feelings and emotions and normal connections, then it would be a simple thing to make him understand. But he didn't. She had no idea how to appeal to this enigma. This immovable rock who looked like a man but didn't behave like one.

She remembered thinking only a few weeks ago that he was heartless. She hated that she was more and more convinced it was true.

She had known him for so many years, and yet didn't know him at all. She knew his body. Knew what made him shake, knew just how to taste him, how to touch him. And she had heard that dark edge that crept into his voice when he spoke about his past, that hinted at the pain he had been through. At how he felt about it all. About what it had done to him. But she could not for the life of her imagine him as a husband. As a father. She knew fragments of him. The boy he had been, the man he was now.

The ruthless and cruel businessman, and the solicitous lover. But those things did not mesh in her mind. She couldn't marry the details together.

She sat in her room for a moment longer, not bothering to change out of her dress, checking her emails and wasting time on the internet until an hour had passed since they'd come home. Then she stood, crossing the room before she had time to fully process what she was doing. Making her way through the penthouse toward his bedroom. She paused at the door, placing her palm on her chest, feeling the raging of her heartbeat beneath her palm. Then she pushed the door open. He was in bed, naked, his blankets pushed down low on his hips, his arm flung up above his head. He was not asleep. He opened his eyes when she opened the door, arching one dark brow. "Yes?"

She crossed the room, climbing onto the bed, staying on top of the covers, lying down next to him.

He shifted, leaning over as though he was going to kiss her. She held up her hand. "No," she said, "I want to talk."

"Well, *agape*, I do not talk in bed."

"You also don't get women pregnant, and you don't ask them to marry you. Given that I already had a couple of exceptions made for me, I would ask that you make one more."

"As you wish," he said, moving back into the position he'd been in when she had come in.

"I want to know you," she said.

He paused. "There is little to know."

"I only knew bits and pieces of your childhood. Whatever you told me. But I'm curious now about all of it. With what I know now, with what you know now, I am curious about everything."

Apollo sighed. "Okay. When I was born, I lived in a

beautiful home. But that did not last. My father worked all the time, and I rarely saw him. Then when I was very young, he lost his position in the company he owned with your father. What was done to him was ruthless, as you know. From there, we lost our home. We lost everything. We lived in…modest housing, to put it mildly."

She wanted to touch him. She had just decided touching was easier than talking, that kissing was easier than honesty. Their bodies were so much easier than anything else. But putting healthy distance between them, she didn't interrupt.

"My father did not take our descent into poverty well. He dealt with his issues by taking drugs, by drinking. Eventually, what little money we had was swallowed up by his addictions. We ended up on the streets. Shortly after that, when he saw what had become of us, when he saw what had become of the family, he killed himself. I will never know why. If he felt ashamed, if he thought we would be better off without him somehow. If he simply didn't want to try anymore. I can never know the answer. And in the end it doesn't matter. The decision was made. The years passed. But one thing I do know is that he would want recompense for what happened to him. For what happened to us."

"That he should have taken himself," she said, the words coming slowly, but with conviction. "If he cared that much he would've stuck around to get revenge himself."

"He couldn't. For whatever reason," he said. "Regardless, my mother and I found ourselves on the streets, then eventually in a horrible group home sort of place. That was when we were sent for. My mother gave very few details, but she said we were going to a new home. Starting over in America. There was a house. Small, I suppose, by some standards. But clean. We wanted for nothing. Suddenly my mother was able to be home with me, instead of desperately searching for work. I had a bed every night."

"I… I can't imagine what that would mean to you in those circumstances."

"I can barely remember. Though it's something I try to hold on to. So that I never forget what it means to be hungry. When you lose the memory of your hunger…you forget why you need success."

She nodded in the darkness. "I know what you mean." She was hungry, too. Not for food or shelter. But for approval she'd never gotten before.

"Your father had come to visit us many times. Sometimes a nanny would be sent to care for me and my mother would go away for a weekend. To be with him, though, I had a boy's understanding. Your father was always good to us. To me. And when he wished to marry my mother, when he spirited us both away to your estate, I thought… I thought we had everything. Suddenly, I gained the world that I had only ever seen glimpses of before."

"I remember you arriving. I was awful to you. Because you scared me. You were…the most beautiful thing I'd ever seen and I knew I shouldn't think that about my stepbrother…like that."

"I suppose not," he said. "You were smart to hold me at a distance, Elle."

"I don't know if *smart* is the word I would use. But it was definitely a defense that worked for a while."

He chuckled. "Yes, it did work for a bit." He paused. "I never asked you… I never asked what it was like to lose your mother like you did. I suppose…your father is as responsible for that as he is for the loss of my father."

The thought made her stomach sink. "I know my father isn't perfect but I have a hard time believing he was so manipulative. But then, I guess maybe I don't... He's a man who likes control, and a man who thinks nothing of pitting his children against each other. So why wouldn't he have always done this, with every person he could? He does it to his own flesh and blood." She moved closer to him, only a bit. "My mother mostly cared about parties and handbags. Lunches with her friends. She was a trophy wife. Her identity was in who my father was, and I suppose that's why I wanted so badly to find something else. To succeed at Matte. To make my own achievements. Except...they were my father's too, really. I was living out my father's plans in my need to please him, in my need to rebel against my mother. I did miss her," she continued. "I really did. Even though I was mostly cared for by nannies. She was my mother, and she smelled of Chanel and vanilla shampoo. And I loved her."

"Of course you did," he said. "My father was distant, a workaholic and an addict, and still I loved him."

"I was happy to have your mother. Mariam has always been good to me."

"But she is not your mother."

Elle's throat tightened. "No. She isn't."

"Nothing can replace what we've lost."

"I guess in a way both of our parents chose to leave us," she said. "Though...my mother could have chosen to come back."

"Or perhaps not. Perhaps she doesn't feel like she can. Not now."

"Maybe. When it became clear the takeover of the company was...hostile... When it became clear you weren't helping...my father put me in control of Matte. And I knew why. I knew it was to use me as a shield. But still, I accepted the position. He's…all I have, really, and I wanted to please him," she said. "I wanted so badly to be accepted. I just wanted him to be proud of me. And then you came in and bought everything out. I thought maybe if I could hold on to my position he would see that I have deserved it all along. But you fired me."

"Had I known your position as CEO was such a contentious one, I might have left you alone."

"I don't know that you would have, Apollo. It isn't in your nature."

"I don't suppose it is."

"I wonder what I would have done," she said, "if he had not selected for me. If I had not been so determined to prove to him that I could be everything that…that you weren't for him."

"You can try and find out, you know. You don't have to go back to work as you. You feel trapped there… There is no reason for you to be there."

"I feel like my team is counting on me. I poured endless hours into it. So much time and energy."

"But you do not have to be there. You are the mother of my child and whatever happens, I will support you financially. You can simply stay home with our child if you prefer. You can go back to school."

She laughed. "I feel like it's too late, really."

"I hope it's never too late to change what you are," he said. "In part because I have been many things in my life. A child of privilege, a gutter snipe, a charity case, wealthy again… We can always change what we are, as long as we stay on earth to breathe one more time."

His words settled heavily on her chest. His father had stopped breathing. And so he had ended his story. "I understand that," she said.

"So if you could do anything, what would you do?"

"I would like to advocate for people who can't do it for themselves. To use the fact that I enjoy challenging people to accomplish something good. A lawyer. But for children, maybe. For women who have been abused."

"That's a very worthy goal," he said.

She shrugged. "It's a fantasy. Anyway, I feel like I was making so much progress with the brand. Really bringing it into the modern era. I know profits aren't off the charts, but the books and cosmetics and the other tie-in products have really taken us to a new level. I want the chance to fight for my staff, for my team."

"Then that is what you will continue to do," he said.

"Why are you doing all this? Saying all this?"

"The baby," he said.

"Of course."

Her eyelids felt heavy now. It was on the tip of her tongue to say that it wasn't really what had brought them together, because he had come back for her before he knew about the child. So she had to wonder what exactly really had. But she was too tired, her brain sluggish, her body even worse.

They had never had a whole conversation without it ending in them yelling at each other or sex. She was almost entirely certain she had never felt comforted by his presence. But she did now. Just being near him. This man who had walked for so long, to gain everything he had.

Everything in her possession had been thrust onto her by her father, whether she wanted it or not. And yes, that came with its own burden. But he had been forced to make the choice to succeed. Yes, her father had paid for his schooling, but if he hadn't taken it seriously, nothing would have come from it.

Had she truly understood the sort of man Apollo was she would have been more terrified of him the first moment he had walked into her company. He was a man who set his sights on things with terrifying single-mindedness. With a kind of intensity unmatched by anyone else she had ever known. If she had realized when he had reappeared in her life that he wanted revenge and he wouldn't hesitate to use her, she would have been much more afraid. Would have behaved much differently with him.

Would you?

Or perhaps, they would be in the same place. In the same moment, in the same bed. Because as much as she wanted to believe she had a bit more common sense, the fact remained that when she fell for him it had nothing to do with common sense.

No, nothing at all. It was so much deeper.

She reached out, resting her palm on his chest, felt his heartbeat beneath her fingertips.

She had dreamed of this. Of simply holding him. Of listening to him breathe. Of sharing the sweet and simple intimacy that came from being near each other. Of touching just to touch.

It felt so good. To simply be with him. Not fighting. Not having sex. Just being.

For the first time in weeks, she felt some peace. She didn't want to sleep. She wanted to prolong this, for as long as possible. If she could choose one moment to stay in, it would be this one.

But sadly, time moved forward. And as it did, she drifted off to sleep.

When they woke in the morning Apollo was still there. Elle had half expected him to have gone off again, to awaken to him standing angrily at the foot of the bed and demanding that she leave. But that didn't happen. Instead, he was wrapped around her, his legs laced through hers. He wasn't wearing any clothes. She was still wearing the dress from last night.

He was awake, and he was looking at her, a strange expression on his face. "Good morning," she said, her voice coming out a little bit like a croak.

"Good morning."

"This is a strange morning after," she said, looking around the room.

"We didn't have sex."

"Yes, that's exactly what I mean."

"How are you feeling?"

"Oh, you mean after…all of that."

He let out a long, heavy breath. "Yes, after I behaved so poorly."

"Wait a second. Are you, Apollo Savas, actually acknowledging the fact that you behaved poorly?"

"Please, don't press the issue, or I will retreat back behind my rock wall of a heart."

"Sometimes I think maybe your secret is that you are not as heartless as you appear." After being convinced of the opposite last night, this was a refreshing feeling.

"We must all maintain our mysteries, must we not?"

"Maybe. I don't think I'm all that mysterious. I think that I reveal myself to you very easily."

"If only that were the case. I should like very much for you to be easier for me to read. And yet, I can't seem to decode you."

"Then you aren't paying attention. The fact that you thought I would crumble at the sight of an engagement ring says that you don't know me very well."

"You never let me."

She let his words take root inside her. They were not untrue. She knew that.

"I know. But after last night you know why. I was afraid. If I had let you touch me at seventeen then we would have been in this position back them. And as poorly as we're handling it now can you imagine how we would have handled it if we were still that young?"

"A nightmare," he said, laughing bitterly. "Yes, it would have been a nightmare."

"I was very afraid of you. Of what you made me feel. I've always been afraid of you." He had the power to devastate her. To tear her apart from the inside out. Apollo possessed so much more dominion over her than she wanted him to know about. Than she would like to admit, even to herself. But the fact of the matter was it had always been so.

"You must not be feeling particularly wonderful, considering you slept in your dress."

She scrubbed at her face. "I suppose I do feel a bit day-old."

"Stay right here." He released his hold on her and got out of bed, crossing the large expanse of the room and heading into the bathroom. She could hear the water start running. Her heart began to beat faster. He was doing something for her. Something thoughtful. Something kind. She wasn't sure how to handle it. So she just lay there, her heart putting a dull, unsteady rhythm in her chest. He returned a moment later, standing in the doorway, naked, and thoroughly unashamed. Of course, he had nothing to be ashamed about. His body was the stuff you could write poetry about.

But she had never been very good with poetry. She would rather lick his body instead. All over. From head to glorious toe, and every muscular inch in between.

Last night, and the no touching, had been... There had been something altering in it. The fact that they had been able to lie together and neither scream at each other nor tear each other's clothes off had been something of a revelation. But that didn't mean she was ready to give up touching him entirely.

Bad idea. You don't even know what kind of relationship the two of you have.

No, she didn't. But if she wanted to move it toward a real relationship, it might be best if she maintained a physical connection with him. At least, that was a handy justification for getting what she wanted. Which was to be back in his strong arms once again. To be brought to the peak of pleasure by his talented hands and mouth.

She shivered.

"If you are cold, *agape*, I have a warm bath for you in here."

For some reason, his tender words made tears prick the back of her eyes. "Okay," she said, standing up on wobbly legs and walking toward him. She paused in front of him and he gripped the hem of her dress, pulling it up over her head. He took over after that, dispensing with her underwear quickly. Then he lifted her up into his arms and set her gently in the deep tub. The water was perfection, as though he had somehow been able to reach down inside of her and figure out exactly what her perfect bath might be like. And then—further proof that he might be reading her mind—he got down into the tub with her, positioning himself behind her, having her press her back up against his broad chest.

"We have not gotten off to the best start. And when I say that, I mean going back more than a decade, we did not have the best start."

She nodded, not saying a word. He ran his hands over her damp skin and she shivered, her nipples tightening and hardened to points in spite of the warmth of the water.

It had nothing to do with temperature, and everything to do with arousal.

"But I think things can be better between us. I'm not… I am not angry at you, Elle. I was, I admit that. I was angry at you for making me want you. For creating a desire within me that I could not satisfy. That was… That was wrong of me."

"Are you apologizing to me?"

"Yes," he said. "I am apologizing to you, because you deserve my apology. I was cruel to you in ways that you did not deserve."

"But my father deserved it," she said, her voice hollow.

"Your father has nothing to do with this. Right now, he has nothing to do with you and me. We can forget that our parents are married. That I feel a sense of betrayal where your father is concerned. We can forget about all of it. Here, right now, we have to do that. Because if we are ever going to bond with one another, if we are ever going to come together and raise this child then there is history we must erase."

"What does that mean? What does it mean for my relationship with my father?"

He reached out and picked up a bottle of shampoo from the edge of the tub, squirting a little bit into his hands. "I don't know." He began to work the lather through her hair, and her heart contracted tightly in on itself. This was what she had wanted, what she had craved all along. This attention. This wonderful, luxurious attention.

He was focused on her now, wholly and completely. In a way that no one else ever had been. It made her want to cry. She would, if she wasn't so afraid of showing that weakness in front of him. Strange how even now, while he was being kind to her, she felt like she had to have her guard up. Like something was still missing.

That made her chest ache. Because she knew it didn't have to be that way. But she didn't know what else they could possibly have, either. They had spent so many years being unkind to each other. Those were the seeds they had planted for their connection, for their relationship. He was right. Maybe all that was left to do was start over. Maybe they had to forget their family. Maybe they had to forget their prior connection. Maybe there was nothing else but this. Maybe that was all there could be. Maybe it was the only way.

She suddenly felt desperate. For him. For his touch, for everything. Suddenly felt like the world would end completely if her mouth wasn't joined to his.

She turned slightly in the water, pressing her hand to his cheek and angling her head, kissing him, slowly, deeply. Trying to make it different from the other times they had kissed. She wanted this to be different. She wanted this to be the new beginning. To be the new start to something that wasn't toxic. To something that wasn't so deadly. Wasn't so dangerous. Maybe it would even be less all-consuming. Maybe it could be something easier. Something freer.

Maybe it would never be a normal relationship, but if he didn't want to use her, and she could trust him…then maybe it could be something.

He was motionless for a moment, as though he was deciding how to react. Then, he gripped her chin with his thumb and forefinger, holding her steady as he deepened the kiss. He kept it slow, too. Tasting her deeply, his pace leisurely as he swept his tongue over hers. As though he really did have all the time in the world. As though they might in fact have forever.

She turned completely, getting on her knees between his size, leaning in, tracing a line on his chest with her tongue, all the way up to his neck where she pressed an openmouthed kiss to his skin. She looked up at him, at the feral light in his eyes, signaling his very tenuous grasp on his control. She affected him. She really did. This had nothing to do with anger, nothing to do with revenge. It was Elle and Apollo, and nothing else in between.

Oh, how she craved that. That connection that was about the two of them and nothing else at all. She moved closer, straddling his lap, bringing the heart of her up against the uncompromising ridge of his arousal. She flexed her hips, rubbing against him, sending a sharp shock of pleasure through her body. He lowered his head, sucking one nipple deeply into his mouth, those two points of pleasure on her body joining up to create a sensation that threatened to overwhelm her completely. She grabbed hold of his face, held him steady, locked her eyes with his as she rose up slightly onto her knees, then lowered herself onto his arousal, taking him deep inside, sighing heavily as he filled her, satisfied her. Completed her.

Apollo Savas had been sex to her from the moment she first met him. From the moment she understood what transpired between a man and a woman in the dark. She had always acknowledged that. Had always known it to be true. But she had missed something. She had missed the most important part of the equation. He wasn't only sex. He was something more. Something deeper. Had it only ever been about sex she would never have been so afraid. But she had known that beneath that desire, beneath that base arousal, was something much darker, much deadlier, much more dangerous.

It had never simply been desire. It had never simply been anger. It was love. It was love then, it was love now.

She loved him. The thought sent a crack of lightning

through her, threatened to split her in two with the pleasure that was building deep inside her. It created a tidal wave of emotion. Completion, satisfaction, despair. She'd never wanted to love him. She had always known that he could never love her back.

No one did. Why would he? Why should Apollo love her for who she was when her own father couldn't do that? When her own mother couldn't seem to manage it? Why should this man ever love her?

And only then could she acknowledge the fact that she had never hated him. Not really. She had loved him.

From the time she was a girl she had loved Apollo Savas. And when he had betrayed her family it had twisted into something new. Because she couldn't understand how the man she cared for so much could do that to her family. When she had thrown herself at him in the hotel room it had been the last gasp of that love, desperate to be heard, desperate to be expressed. And when she had said she hated him it was only because hate was the other side of that coin. So close to love. So perilously close, she understood now. Because it was love twisted, turned into something ugly.

She realized then, as Apollo looked down at her with his dark eyes glittering, that he had loved her father. That he had loved her family, and that was why it had been twisted into this. That was why, in the beginning, he had gone so far to seek his revenge. To use her. To harm her.

Because of how love could get twisted up.

He gripped her hips hard, taking control of their movements, thrusting up inside her, chasing his release. And she was grateful, because she had gone weak. She could no longer take control of this, no longer claim control over this interaction. No, she was now at the mercy of it. At the mercy of him, at her desire for him.

He slid his hand around to cup her bottom, gripping her tightly, his fingertips brushing up against where they joined. That added bit of contact was enough to send her over the edge. Her mind went blank for one glorious moment, pleasure stealing over her, rocking her like a crack of thunder.

And when it was over, when it all settled, when she was still straddling him, their eyes on only each other, pleasure coursing through her like an endless wave, there was only one bright, brilliant thought in her mind.

She loved Apollo Savas. She always had, she had a suspicion she always would. And she knew, with just as much certainty, that he would never love her in return.

CHAPTER TWELVE

ELLE HAD BEEN quiet ever since they had woken up that morning. Or, more specifically, ever since he had given her a bath. He could feel her slipping out of his grasp. Even as they had reached the peak together, he had felt her pull away, and he didn't know what to do about that. He didn't even know what he thought about it. If it mattered. Except that for Elle, he had a feeling emotion mattered. That it was key.

He could take or leave it. He wanted nothing more than a connection based on honesty, on a contract. It was why he wanted marriage. He wanted to have a guarantee.

He didn't trust emotions. Not in the least. Not when his mother had led such a tangled existence based on the men who had professed to love her. Not when the man who had behaved most like a father to him had revealed himself to be the worst sort of liar. How could he even fathom putting stock in emotion under those conditions?

But Elle was most certainly a more emotional creature. If only he could figure out how to read her. If only he could figure out how to connect with her. He had tried talking, he had tried kindness. And then, she had initiated sex. Neither was the magic key. He wasn't sure there was a damn magic key. He found that disconcerting.

He walked around the expensive penthouse, learning the layout of his new home. Regardless of what he had said to her earlier about how much time he would spend with her and the child, he was anticipating trying to accomplish most of his work in the States, from now on. His own father had abandoned him through suicide. His stepfather had proven to be an imposter. He would not have his child living life with that sort of cloud over them. Money only solved certain things. He knew that for a fact. Coming out of poverty and into financial gain had shown him that there were still things that money couldn't buy.

If only Elle's undying affection was one of the things money could buy. It would make things much simpler. Instead, he was left trying to untie one of the great mysteries of the modern age, or any age. Feminine emotion.

As he was brooding on this, his phone buzzed in his pocket. He picked up quickly without bothering to look and see who it was. "Savas."

"What the hell are you doing with my daughter?"

It was the voice of his least favorite devil on the end of the line. "That depends on what you've heard."

"I have seen the headline in this morning's society pages. You proposed to her last night at a restaurant. By all accounts she refused you and stormed out."

"Then I fail to see why you're calling me. Obviously Elle is up to the challenge of handling herself."

"I am calling because I feel that I have the right to know exactly what led you to a place where you thought proposing to my daughter might end in a *yes*. Do not tell me you set yourself up for public humiliation on purpose, Apollo. I would not believe it."

"It's almost as though you know me," he said, his tone easy. "I had thought she might say yes."

"After all I have done for you—"

"Yes, after causing the suicide of my father, after blackmailing my mother into a relationship, how dare I not be more grateful?"

"I hardly orchestrated your father's death, Apollo, as you are well aware. Your father made his own choices. I was certainly ruthless in my desire to push him out of the company, but what happened after that was his choice, not mine."

"In my mind, you pulled the trigger. There is nothing on earth that will convince me otherwise."

"And so you're using Elle to get revenge?"

It was on the tip of his tongue to tell him that's exactly what he was doing. To let the older man know that Apollo had corrupted his only daughter. That he had gotten her with child. That he now held all the power. It all belonged to him. But then, she walked into the room, wearing soft, baggy pants, and a loose-fitting top. Looking soft and vulnerable, not the least bit hard and glamorous. And he realized that he could not say those things. He could not use her that way. She had asked him to see her as a woman, and he did. He had been the one to suggest they put it all behind them, to start new. And so, he would choose to do so. Now, he would choose to do it for her. For them.

"Whether you believe it or not, my association with your daughter has nothing to do with you."

Elle's head snapped in his direction, her eyes rounded.

"I don't believe it," David said.

"That is inconsequential. It is the truth. I intend to win her over, one way or another. I will obtain her hand in marriage."

"Why is it so important to you?"

"Because I want her."

"And you love her?"

The question hit its mark like an arrow striking a target. Nearly made him fall to his knees. He thought about love, what it meant to him. Certainly, his mother loved him, in her way. She was a fragile woman, not unsurprising considering all she had been through. And at times he wondered if she simply had no choice but to detach in order to protect herself from further pain. After the loss of her husband, after being blackmailed into marrying a man she had not chosen.

His father, his biological father, had been so consumed with the acquisition of material things, with his status, that he had preferred death over staying and protecting his wife and child. In that sense, Apollo could not deny David's words. Suicide had been his father's choice. And not anyone else's. Though he knew that there were many complicated factors that played into that. Depression, mental torments that he could not possibly understand.

It did not stop him from retaining a boy's perspective on it in many ways. He felt abandoned. He felt angry. Whether or not his father deserved more sympathy than that was irrelevant. Apollo could only feel what he felt.

And then there was David St. James. He had truly taken him in. Truly accepted him as part of the family.

He had been a father to him. More of a father than his own had ever been. He had raised him, taught him the value of hard work, paid for his education, taught him to take nothing for granted. Though he was a hard man, though he was distant at times, he was a solid, steady figure in Apollo's life. The man he had sought to pattern himself after. Discovering the depths he had sunk to in order to obtain Apollo's mother—as though she were an item to be acquired and not a human being, as though Apollo himself and his father were incidentals—that had shown him just how deep a lie could run.

The fact that his feelings for the older man had not been eradicated overnight—if ever—showed him just what a fickle and dishonest emotion love could be.

Worse still, all of that, every bit of it, was proof that his love twisted things. Changed them in permanent and ugly ways. He was like a lit match brought up against the edge of something fragile. Making the edges curl and darken, altered beyond recognition.

He couldn't do that to her. He wouldn't.

"No," he said. "No, I don't."

"Then you don't deserve her."

And with that, the line went dead. Those words echoed in his head as he turned to look at Elle, who was regarding him with a confused expression. "My father?"

"Yes. He is unamused with me."

"Did he see it in the paper? Was it in the paper?"

"Yes," he said. "Apparently your rejection of me has made headlines."

"Well, I would apologize but it really is your own doing."

"This is true."

"What did he ask you?"

"He asked if you were my revenge," Apollo said. "I told him you're not."

"Yes, I gathered as much. But what was the last question he asked you?"

His stomach tightened, dropped low in his midsection. "He asked me if I loved you."

She closed her eyes, her face going pale. "You said no."

Elle felt as though the ground was dropping out from beneath her feet. She had been shocked, thrilled, when Apollo had not taken the chance to eviscerate her father. When he had not used her as a weapon. Had not trotted out the baby, their affair, in a crass and unnecessary way. That when he had been asked directly if he was using her, he had said no. Even if it was a lie, even in part, he had stopped using her then. He had honored her request.

But then he had been asked if he loved her. And his answer had been no.

She realized then that it was nonnegotiable for her. She needed love. She needed for him to love her. There was nothing more important. Nothing at all.

She had dressed it up in all kinds of fancy descriptions. Had tried to convince herself that all she needed was respect. That they needed to find common ground. That she simply needed someone to want her as she was, and not as a weapon in some kind of scheme. But after their encounter in the bath, after that pleasure radiated through her, after she had felt the intensity of her own feelings for him, she knew that that wasn't the case. She needed more. She needed everything. And anything else would be doing herself a terrible disservice.

She wanted more for herself. More than simply heading up a company because she wanted to prove to her father that she could. More than marriage to a man for his convenience. In truth, as much as she wanted to give her child a home with both parents she knew that if they were living together under sufferance, if she made him miserable because he eventually bored of her, and he made her miserable because her love went unreturned, their child would know. He or she would sense the unhappiness, and for them to even suspect that their presence was the cause of that kind of relationship was something she could not place upon her child.

"I can't marry you," she said.

"What are you talking about? You showed me this morning just how irresistible you find me."

"That's sex, Apollo. We have had that through everything. When I was terrible to you, you still wanted me. When you took over my business, betrayed our family, I still wanted you. Even while I was thinking about stabbing you through the chest with a pen, I wanted you. But that isn't enough for marriage. And right now? It isn't enough for me. I realized something this morning."

"That you are a contrary little thing who makes absolutely no sense?"

"That I love you. I love you with everything I have. It has always been that way. But I cannot, and will not, continue to accept this strange, leftover existence that I have cobbled together with the discarded pieces of yours and my father's manipulative plans. I'm the CEO at Matte because he wanted to play me against you, not because he thought I was suited to the position. I'm pregnant with your baby because you wanted to hurt him, and while I appreciate the fact that you didn't rub it in his face just now...that's our foundation. It's what we are."

"No," he said, his voice rough. "That is not our foundation. There was no calculation when I took you up against the wall in my hotel room, no ulterior motive when I had you in the elevator."

"How can I believe that?"

"Because it is the truth. I decided after I had you the second time that I would use what was between us to get revenge. Only because I was desperate to find some justification for what you did to me. For wanting to indulge in this thing between us."

"And why'd you come back?"

"Because I wasn't finished with you!"

"But that's the thing," she said. "I am not a thing that you can pick up and put down at your convenience. Not a weapon that you can use at your discretion. I am a human being. I have feelings. I love you and I deserve to be loved in return." She shook her head. "If you cannot give me that then I will have to go out and find someone who can."

All of the anger drained from his face, his expression turning to stone. "You are correct. If that is what you want, then that is what you must find."

Her chest felt hollowed out, her heart thundering hard in the empty space. "That's it?"

"We are at an impasse, Elle. I cannot love, and you require it. I do not wish to hold you prisoner. I see no satisfaction in making you miserable. There was a time when I might have, but things have changed."

"Maybe that means you have feelings for me?"

"No," he said, his tone hard, definitive. "I cannot."

She felt like she'd been stabbed clean through, like she would bleed out on the floor, her pain, her love, everything for him to see. She wouldn't be able to hide anymore, as she had done for so many years.

She waited for something to come, for a cutting remark to rescue her, but it wasn't there. There was nothing to hide behind. Nothing but pain and love in equal measure.

And she wanted him to see it. Wanted him to know. She was done hiding. She'd done enough damage pushing him away so that she wouldn't be hurt.

She had hidden everything for years. Her pain, her desire, her love. And she was done. Pride be damned, she wouldn't hide herself anymore.

"Why?" she asked. "Why are you doing this? There is nothing stopping us, nothing stopping this except you, and I can't understand why."

"Everything I love turns to dust, Elle. I would not have you so diminished."

"I've been diminished already!" she shouted. "All of my life. To keep the peace, to try and do what my father wanted, to try and avoid…well, exactly this, with you." She swallowed hard, shaking, all of her repressed emotion, decades of it, pouring out now. "I'm done with that. I'm making demands now."

He stared at her for a moment, his dark eyes hollow. "I can't meet them."

"You won't."

"It amounts to the same thing."

And then he turned away from her, and walked out of the penthouse, closing the door softly behind him. She had a feeling that he would not be back.

She didn't want half a life, half a love. She didn't want a future with a man who wouldn't give her what she'd just realized she so desperately wanted.

So, she let him go. And she did her very best not to cry.

Elle approached her father's office with great trepidation. She was going to let him know that she was officially resigning from Matte. She was also going to tell him about the baby, and the fact that she would not be marrying Apollo. She took a deep breath, trying to ease the knot in her chest. Then, she raised her hand and knocked on the door.

"Come in."

She turned the knob and opened the door, stepping inside quickly. "Hello, Father," she said.

"Elle," he said, gesturing at the chair across from his desk, as though she were a business appointment he was keeping. "Have a seat."

She did. "I imagine you're wondering why I wanted to speak with you."

"Not particularly. I assume it has something to do with Apollo."

"Well," she said, "you aren't wrong."

"Have you decided to marry him?"

"On the contrary, I have decided that I cannot continue my association with him."

"I fail to understand why there was an association with him in the first place. He turned against me."

"Yes," she said.

"He fired you. Then, you got your job back, did you not?"

Her face got hot. "I know what you're implying, but it didn't happen that way. Anyway, I'm stepping down at Matte. I'm going to go back to school. I'm going to figure out what *I* want to do. Quite apart from your expectations, or his. I have been caught in the cross fire for too long. I just can't do it anymore. I have to find out what I am beyond this…desperate people pleaser. I have to find out if I can be more than your shield to block you from Apollo's wrath."

"Is that what you think?"

"Why would I think anything else?" she asked.

"And yet, you have never said anything."

"Yes, well, I wanted to keep the peace. I wanted to do the right thing, be the daughter you needed. But I'm over that now. I need to be the person I'm happy with, not the person you're happy with."

"Did I force you into the position at Matte?" he asked, his tone hard.

"You can't deny that you used me to try and stand between Apollo and the destruction of the company. It had nothing to do with me. You never intended to give any of it to me. You always wanted a son, and until he went rogue, Apollo was that son for you. I was never supposed to be the one in that position. You used me."

He lifted his shoulder, the lines on his face looking suddenly more pronounced. "Yes, I did use you. But how else could I defend my legacy? I knew you could do it, Elle. I had no concerns about that. I knew Apollo had... feelings for you. Feelings of some kind, and I thought that perhaps he would modify his actions if you were in the line of fire."

"And so you used me as a target."

"I knew you were strong enough. You might think it's because I don't respect or value you, but it is to the contrary. You're strong. I would not have shielded a son from such a thing, and I did not shield you."

"Am I supposed to be grateful?"

"I could see no other way," he said, his tone uncompromising.

"Is that why you ousted Apollo's father from your company all those years ago? Because you could think of no other way to be with Mariam?"

"Yes," he said, simply. Calmly. "It was the only way I could think of to win Mariam. And so I did what I could. But she stood by him. Had his child. And for all my sins, I never held that against Apollo. That he was the product of a union I despised."

"You don't get a medal for that, Dad," she said. "Not when you were so...horrible."

"I was horrible," he said, his tone hard, his eyes ice blue. "And I would do the same thing again. Make the same choices. I didn't intend for his father to kill himself, Elle. I am not a mind reader. I could not predict the outcome. I did, however, think that it was likely Mariam would leave him when he had nothing and I had everything. I was wrong."

"She loved him."

Her father nodded slowly. "Yes, she did. But she has learned to love me, I think."

"You think?"

"Yes. I do."

"Have you ever asked her?"

Her father's face went blank. "No. I haven't. But then, I'm not certain it matters. Not now."

Elle's heart crumpled. "I think it always matters. It doesn't matter when love comes, as long as you know it's there. Does she know you love her?"

"I destroyed her world to move her into mine. I cleared my world to make room for her. If that is not love then I do not know what is."

He didn't. Elle could see that. He truly and honestly knew nothing of love being two-sided. Of giving rather than taking.

He was an unbending man. Unyielding. All arrogance and a stiff neck. Unable to truly turn and look at anyone else.

"I think perhaps love isn't destroying worlds. Or moving people around like chess pieces," she said, her voice shaking. "I think maybe it's giving more than you take. Showing it, even when someone may never show it back. Being kind even when the other person is cruel. I think love isn't always balance, but if both are willing to give more than they take…it might be a beautiful, rare sort of treasure."

"I don't know about any of that, Elle," he said. "I do know that I have you, and I still have Mariam. In that I find some success, I think."

"Do you love *me*?" She might as well ask. She had already been rejected by Apollo, so there was really no reason to protect herself at this point. She had been flayed already. She might as well allow some salt to be rubbed into the wounds.

Her father only looked at her for a moment, his gaze unreadable. "Did you not know?" he asked.

"How would I?" she answered.

"I am your father, Elle."

"That doesn't make any guarantees."

"I am a man who has built my life on a foundation made of ruthless decisions. I did not become rich by following the rules. I did not obtain my wife by playing fair. I hurt Hector. I hurt your mother. I have never known quite how to handle the people in my life. But for all of that, I do love you."

It was still indirect. Still impersonal. But she felt it was very likely the best he could do.

She also saw, for a moment, herself in the old man's gaze. Waiting to be given what she wanted, all of her conditions met. No, she wasn't being unreasonable wanting love from Apollo. But she had to consider where he had come from. What he knew.

Apollo had been broken. Battered by life. People he had trusted had abandoned him. Betrayed him. He needed someone to show him something different. Needed someone to stand by him, no matter what. To take what he could give now, and trust there would be more in the future.

She would do that for him. For her. Just because he couldn't meet her here now didn't mean he never would.

She loved him. She would love him enough for them both.

"I love you," she said, because she thought she might as well practice saying it again, to another man who had difficulty hearing it, saying it. To continually practice this new start, where she didn't hide. Where she didn't try to make herself palatable. "In spite of everything."

"I haven't changed," he said. "I am the man you have always known. You just know a bit more of the story."

"Yes, well, the whole story is important. It doesn't mean I think you made good choices."

"I never asked anyone to sign off on my choices. I made my bed, and it has the woman I love in it. How can I have regrets?"

"Well," Elle said, "I'm going to go after the man I love now. Because he's pigheaded and stubborn and scared. And I'm okay with that. As long as I can be with him. Oh. I'm having his baby, also. That might be relevant, too."

That seemed to successfully shock her father. His gray eyebrows shot upward, his mouth dropping slightly open. "You didn't see fit to mention that sooner?"

"We got philosophical. I imagine this will be the only time. But... Apollo is the father of my child. You're married to his mother, you're both the grandparents of the baby." She frowned. "It's very complicated. And you're going to have to make some kind of peace with him."

"It may not be possible. As you said, the whole story changes things. And for him, I think it transformed me into a villain. One I cannot deny I have been in years past. I tried to make it up to him by giving him all I could. But as you have pointed out to me, my demonstrations are not always clear."

"You've both caused a lot of damage. Fighting, seeking vengeance, going after what you want with no care for others...it just has to stop. If it can't be anything more than a cease-fire then let it be that. But it has to stop. I can't be in the middle. I won't allow my child to be in the middle."

"And if you have to choose between me or him?"

"It would be him," she said, not even hesitating. "Assuming he felt the same way."

Her father nodded slowly, his lips curving into a smile. "Maybe you even understand my more ruthless decisions."

"Where Apollo is concerned I have no doubt I could be ruthless. Where my child is concerned... I would shed blood."

"I fear I was too selfish to make that choice," her father said. "And that I did not have the pride that you do."

"What do you mean?"

"I did not care if Mariam felt as strongly as I did. I only cared that I had her."

"Well, I lived too much of my life that way and I won't do it now."

Her father regarded her with...pride. For the first time she could honestly say she felt it. A strange moment because she didn't feel particularly triumphant. She only felt...broken. Sad. Pride was a poor salve for a broken heart.

"I need to be loved," she repeated, for herself as much as anyone. "And I need to be assured that my son or daughter will not be used as a pawn. Not for Apollo to hurt you, not for him to hurt me. I think you will find my love for my child the most ruthless of all."

"Then go," her father said. "Tell him. Go and be ruthless for love."

CHAPTER THIRTEEN

APOLLO WAS NO stranger to despair. While he had not been terribly conscious of the loss of wealth as a boy, the loss of his comfortable bedroom, his bed, had certainly been things he'd felt deeply. After that, the loss of his father. Then, the loss of the man he had come to think of as a father.

But he had never once experienced loss like this. A loss that was, in many ways, his own doing. There had been no control in his hands when they had lost their livelihood and their money, there had been no control when he had discovered the true nature of David St. James. But here... With Elle, he'd held the power. The power to tell her what she wanted to hear, to find a way to be the man she needed. And he had turned away.

"Coward," he said aloud to the empty space in his office. He paced in front of the window, looking out over the city below. He had gone back to Greece, because he had not known what else to do. Had not known where else to go. He felt helpless, and it had been a long time since he had felt helpless. He despised the feeling. More than anything. It was one of the many reasons he had turned so sharply, so hard, on David St. James.

Because when the revelation had struck him it'd been with the force of a killing blow. It had chopped his legs out from beneath him, left him gasping, shocked. He was not a man who took kindly to such a thing.

Wounded pride, Apollo? That is a very small reason to seek revenge. A very small reason to hold on to anger.

But what his father had been through... What his mother had been through...

He knew he should speak to his mother. But the simple fact was he was afraid to hear what she had to say. He had been from the moment three years ago when the revelations about David had become clear. He didn't want to hear what she had to say. For fear that she loved him. For fear that she was happy. For fear that she supported the decisions her new husband had made because it had resulted in the two of them being together.

But he knew now that he needed to ask her. He knew that he needed to find out why she had stayed.

He picked up the phone, dialing her number, dimly aware that it was very early in the morning in New York. "Hello?"

His mother's faintly accented voice came over the line. "Hello, Mother," he said.

They had barely spoken over the course of the past three years, and when they had, it had been very carefully. Because she had known that he was actively pursuing vengeance against her husband, and while she had kept her feelings to herself, he could always sense the fact that she didn't approve. Certainly, she didn't necessarily support him, as she had not demanded he take her with him, back to Greece. He was more than capable of supporting his mother now. She did not have to stay with David St. James. And yet, she did.

"Why?" he asked, with no preamble at all. He had not meant to launch straight into it like this, but he had been unable to help himself.

"Why what, Apollo?"

"Why do you stay with him? I don't understand. The truth about David St. James was hidden from me for all of my life. But it was not hidden from you. You knew exactly what manner of man he was. And yet, you remain with him. You could leave. I could take care of you until the end of time, and you would never want for anything."

There was silence on the other end. "Yes," she said softly. "I do know what manner of man he is. I have known David St. James since long before you were born. I knew him from the beginning. I met him when I met your father. I don't know why, but I have a tendency to love hard men. Though perhaps that is a good thing for you, I think."

Apollo chuckled. "I suppose it is."

"I did love your father. And I stayed with him even when we lost everything. Even when David ousted him from the company."

"Which David did to hurt him."

Mariam continued as if he hadn't spoken. "I do believe that at the time, your father already had a bit of an issue with drugs. Though they had not yet consumed him as they did later. He was working long hours, and he needed something to help him keep up. It was competitive. He didn't want to sleep. I rarely saw him. And I would be… I would be lying if I said we were perfectly happy. But I was never unfaithful to him. I knew that David had feelings for me. But I had chosen Hector. And so I remained with him. I remained with him until the end, when everything became so twisted, and so hard. By the time he died he was not the man I had first known."

"Because of David St. James."

"Yes, and no. Business is harsh and uncompromising.

It has always been so. Many men lose all their earthly possessions and come out the other side."

Apollo was having trouble processing what she was saying. "You're saying you harbor no anger against him over what he put us through?"

"I am sorry to tell you that I put much more of the blame at your father's door than I do at David's. Yes, he ousted him from the company, but had your father taken better care of our assets we would not have been destitute. Had he not completely given up, we could have come back from it. I had no skills. I was nothing more than a village girl who knew how to do little more than sew. And while that could support us in a very modest fashion it was never going to pull us out of poverty. When David contacted me… I am not proud of what happened after that, because for all of my sins, for all of my divided loyalty, the one thing that I truly regret was any part I might have played in the destruction of his marriage."

Apollo swallowed hard. It was difficult to hear such things. To take on the knowledge of his own mother's part in all of this. "Yes, well, you had a child to take care of."

"He did not force me into an affair," she said, her voice soft. "That was my choice. When he discovered how we were living he asked us to come, he offered to buy me a house, and to care for you. A relationship was not part of that. But I… I was lonely. And I recognized what I might have had. I regretted not choosing him, I think. Because he seemed stronger. That was my mistake, Apollo. His as well, but do not blame it all on him."

"Well, his ex-wife didn't care enough about her own child to stick around after she was deposed."

His mother sighed. "No, she did not. Again, it does not excuse my actions. But I do love Elle, almost as if she were my own."

"She knows that."

"I hope so. There was a time when I thought you knew that David loved you as a son, as well."

"I did believe that," Apollo said. "But when I found out the level he had stooped to to bring you to him, to get revenge because of his love being spurned, I could not simply stay in his home, stay as his son."

"It is done," she said. "It may have been wrong, but it is done."

"I loved him," Apollo said. "What kind of a son does that make me? I cannot love without it becoming something horribly twisted. You had to care for me, and that forced your hand. I loved my father, but it wasn't enough to make him stay... David..."

"None of this, none of the tangled web, is your fault. You should not place more consequences onto yourself. We were badly behaved adults, who got our children caught in the cross fire of terrible games. Neither of you deserved it. I wish very much your father had not killed himself. But he was not simply a victim, either. Your love didn't bring out the worst in us, Apollo. Your love was the best of us."

He swallowed hard, his throat suddenly tight. "None of it is simple," he said. "None of it. So I do not understand how I am supposed to sort through it all."

"I can't answer that question for you. I do know that it doesn't benefit anyone to hold on to anger. To hold on to the past. It twists you. That's what it did to Hector. It broke him completely. All of the anger that he felt toward David... I would hate for you to suffer the same fate."

"And so...you would simply forgive?"

"I cannot make the decision for you, Apollo. I should like, for the sake of our family, for you to find it in you to forgive. But it is your journey. Perhaps I was wrong to forgive. I do not know. I only know that I had choices before me and I took the one that made me happiest."

"We can never be a family as we were," he said, "in part because while you may love Elle as a daughter, I do not love her as a sister."

That declaration was met with silence. "I know," she said finally. "I have always known."

Those words nearly broke him. Shattered him entirely. She had always known, because his feelings had always been there. Every action, every cruelty, all the anger that had passed between them over the years had been there simply to disguise that fact.

From himself.

He had never managed to hide it from his mother.

"I do not know how I can be with her."

"We can only carry so much, Apollo. I have lived an imperfect life, and if I have learned anything it's that, at some point, we must put some of our burdens down so we can pick up things we would more gladly carry. These are decisions we make. We cannot wait for the pain to go away. We cannot simply expect the anger to fade, or the grief to stop biting. We must make choices. They are the hardest choices to make. But if you want to move on, then you must begin on your own."

"That simple?"

"No," she said. "That difficult."

"I know what I want," he said. "I just don't know if I can have it."

"You're angry at David, and that is understandable. You want revenge, and that I understand, as well. But I think you can see the way that revenge twists your own life. If you deny your love for Elle simply because you want to punish David St. James, then it isn't truly him you're hurting. Then the only person whose life you've destroyed is your own."

"You stayed because you love him?"

"God help me, but I do," she said. "Though I should not. Though he perhaps doesn't deserve it. There are many days when I don't deserve it, either. Though, in his way, I believe he loves me."

He could not say he envied his mother her relationship, her marriage. And yet, he could see that they had love for each other, even if it wasn't the sort he recognized. And what sort did he recognize? That, he supposed, was the question. Did he recognize it at all?

He had. With Elle, he had recognized it for the first time. And he had run, because it had been too much. Because, as his mother said, he was carrying too much anger to accept the love that she was asking for, that she was offering.

"I suppose I have a decision to make," he said.

But it was already made. There was no question. He loved Elle. And that meant whatever the risk, whether he was able to trust himself or not, whether he truly believed he knew how to love and how to accept love, he wanted to give her what he could. What he had. He wanted to give her everything. "I will have to get her back," he said finally.

"I hope that you do," his mother said. "I hope it isn't too late."

He hung up the phone and turned back to the sprawling city before him. He would need to get the first plane out. Or perhaps he should call her. But he didn't know if apologies such as this one should be done over the phone. He had hurt her, had said terrible things. Hurtful things. He did not deserve to ask forgiveness. But dammit, if David St. James could earn the love of the woman he wanted after all he had done, why couldn't Apollo?

He turned back to the door of his office just as it opened. In strode Elle, looking red-faced, pursued by his assistant Alethea.

"I'm sorry, Mr. Savas," Alethea said. "She insisted that she had to see you."

"I do," Elle said, looking stubborn. He adored that expression. That uncompromising, demanding expression. Elle was not an easy woman. She never would be. But he didn't want easy. He wanted her. Always. Forever.

"It's okay, Alethea. I would like to see her."

Alethea shook her head. "Best you work out your problems, Mr. Savas. You have been mercurial of late, and I find it irritating," she said, turning on her heel and storming out of his office.

"That is not the sort of assistant I expected you to have," Elle said.

"Yes, well. At this point she knows where all the bodies are buried and I can't get rid of her. Sadly, she knows that."

"I had to see you," she said.

"Why is that, *agape*?"

"Because I have something to tell you."

Suddenly, his stomach plummeted. "It isn't about the baby, is it?"

"The baby is fine," she said.

"I'm relieved to hear it."

"It isn't about that. I mean, it is. But nothing is wrong."

"Well, before you launch into your speech, I must tell you, I was on my way back to see you."

"You were?"

"Yes," he said, "I was. There is something I need to tell you to. I spoke to my mother this morning."

"That's funny. I spoke to my father about… Well, I guess it must be fifteen hours ago or so. Since I am here now."

"I see. I needed to understand why she stayed with him. I needed to understand how she had managed to let go of everything that had gone on in the past. She helped clarify some things. For one, your father did not force her into a relationship. That is important for me to know. She admits they handled things poorly. But he did not force her."

Elle looked visibly relieved by the revelation. "I'm glad to hear that. That isn't something my father would willingly admit. He's such a stubborn old man. I think talking about his feelings is the thing he dislikes most in the world. But he did admit to me… He does love your mother. For all of his sins, he does."

"She loves him," Apollo said. "Somehow, she was able to let go of everything that had happened all those years ago. Somehow she fell in love with him."

"We don't have half of that baggage standing between us, and here we are unable to sort out our differences."

"There's a simple enough reason for that," he said. "I was a coward."

"You're not a coward, Apollo."

"Yes, I am. I was unable to admit my feelings for you nine years ago, and I found myself unable to admit them last week. Even to myself. But I love you, Elle. I always have."

Elle could only stand there, shocked, staring into Apollo's intense, dark gaze. He said that he loved her. He said that he always had, that he had simply been unable to admit it. That was not what she'd been expecting. She had flown to Athens, stormed into his office expecting a fight. Expecting to engage him in a knock-down, drag-out battle as she told him there would be no revenge. That they would be putting everything aside for love. Not theirs, but the love of their child. And yet, here he was…saying he loved her.

"I had a speech prepared," she said, her voice sounding hollow.

"Did you?" he asked, his eyebrows arched.

"Yes," she said. "I was… I was going to make sure you knew that our child was everything. That I would never use a child to get revenge on you, nor would I allow you to use our child to hurt me. And that under no circumstances would I allow our son or daughter to be caught in the crosshairs of your issues with my father."

"There is no danger of that."

"I… I see that. Because you… But I…" She suddenly felt a sharp pain in her chest. "I'm sorry."

"For?"

"You do love me. I knew you did. I really did. But I didn't trust it."

"Why should you take less than you deserve, Elle? Why should you take less than you deserve simply waiting around for me?"

"Because love isn't about what you deserve."

"Thankfully for me," he said.

"For all of us. We're about to have a child, and we're evidence of the fact that…parents make mistakes with their children. Even children they love."

"That is true."

"Love is…bigger than keeping score. It costs more than we could ever hope to earn. At least, it's supposed to. I need you to know, here and now, that I love you without reservations. That I believe you *do* love me. I understand what you've been through. I understand that you were used badly." She took a deep breath. "Your mother may have been able to easily forgive my father, or at least forgave him eventually, but she knew everything from the beginning. Your trust was betrayed in a way that hers wasn't."

Apollo shook his head. "The guilt that I felt over considering David a father figure to me was what truly enraged me."

"I recognized that. That what you felt was badly-used love. I did. Because I had experienced it with you. But even recognizing that, I was unbending."

"I want you to be unbending, my sweet, beautiful Elle," he said.

Her chest swelled, her heart feeling large and tender. "You do?"

"Yes. Because I want everything you are. Everything you will be. Because I want the woman you are, not simply the woman that makes my life easiest. I do not want you simply because you are the mother of my child. I do not want you because you are biddable, because you fit easily into the life I have created. I will rearrange it all for you," he said. "Somehow, I think I knew I would have to do that. And it frightened me. Again, you must understand that I am a coward."

She shook her head. "No," she said, the word coming out broken. "You are the bravest man I have ever known. Because you would open yourself up to love again even when your love had been so abused before."

"I hardly deserve a medal for accepting a gift so beautiful as your love," he said.

"Yours is beautiful too, you know."

His chest pitched sharply, his dark eyes glittering. "I was so convinced my love killed things. That it was toxic. How could I trust something that always turned into something so painful? So I denied it. What I felt for you. It was always there. I wrapped it up in anger, I wrapped it up in hate, because I wasn't ready to reach out and take it."

"I did the same," she said, her throat tight. "I told myself that I hated you, that I couldn't stand the sight of you, because in truth you were the most glorious, wonderful sight I had ever beheld. And I called my feelings something else, anything else, rather than accepting the fact that I might never have you. I pretended I didn't care rather than opening myself up and risking being humiliated. Rather than risking admitting what I might lose and how badly it might hurt. I hid my feelings, even from myself. See, I am more like my father than it seems on the surface."

"But you're here. You're here telling me now."

"If we can't learn from the mistakes of the people who came before us, then I fail to see the point of any of it."

"Yes." He shook his head. "You are very right about that. When I look at the mistakes my mother made, your father made, that my father made, in their pursuit of love, of money and success, I see nothing but a sad, tangled web. And in the end, I suppose what our parents have found is love, as best as they can have it."

"Yes," Elle said. "I think that's true."

"But I want more than that. I want deeper. None of the anger, none of the pride, none of those wasted years."

Elle laughed softly. "I suppose we already have a few wasted years."

"But no more. It is you for me, Elle. Only you. I want to make a life with you. With you and our child. I will get down on my knees and beg if I must, because my pride is nothing more than dirt if it keeps me from you."

"As enjoyable as I might find that, I don't need you to

beg. I love you already. I don't need you to do anything to gain that acceptance."

He crossed the space between them and her heart lurched, a thrill racing through her as he took her into his arms. This would never fade. It would never get old. Things had never been hotter, more intense between them because of the anger. The anger had simply covered the true intensity. It was only bigger now. Brighter, deeper. Now that she knew the racing of her heart, the intense surge of adrenaline that raced through her every time she saw him was not hate, but love after all.

"I love you," he said. "And I will lay down all of my anger, my need for revenge, my distrust and anything else that might hinder my ability to give you all that you deserve. Because if I am to be full, then I would have myself be full of nothing but my love for you."

"I was so hurt, Apollo, because I was afraid that you wanted me only for revenge. To hurt other people. And I never felt like my father loved me for *me*. I never felt like anyone in my life loved me simply because of who I am. But here you are, asking me to be difficult, asking me to be stubborn, asking for me to be myself. And I... I can hardly believe it."

"Then I will spend my every day, from this moment until the end, showing you just how much I love you, for all of the good, all of the bad and everything in between. I will do my very best to ensure that you never doubt that you are the one I love. You are the one I want. Whether you're a CEO, a lawyer, a cupcake maker, a police officer."

"I have never given any indication that I want to be a baker or a police officer."

"But you could be. You could be anything you wanted

to be, and you would still be Elle. And I would still love you."

"There is a remarkable amount of freedom in that," she said, her chest swelling with emotion. "I don't think you can possibly know what that means to me."

He pulled her closer, kissing her lips. "Then show me, Elle. Show me."

EPILOGUE

SHE DID. AND she spent every day after that showing him, demonstrating her love for him. And he did the same for her.

It was one of Apollo's proudest moments when Elle graduated at the top of her law class. One of his happiest moments, sitting there, cheering her on as she walked onstage while he held their daughter in his lap, with their new baby in the crook of his other arm. He was so proud of what she had achieved, of what she had decided to go after. Of how she had decided to use her uncompromising nature and sharp tongue.

She was, in his opinion, the best lawyer in New York City, eternally advocating for women in difficult circumstances, and for children who had had injustice done against them.

If someone would have told him when he had first married Elle that he would only grow to love her more over the next decade, he would have told them they were insane. After all, how could anyone love more than he had on the day of his wedding? But he discovered just how deep, just how wide, love could grow. Each year, each child, each achievement and each failure added a texture and a richness to what he felt for her that stretched far beyond what he could have ever imagined.

On the night of their tenth anniversary, Elle came home from work, exhausted, frowning, possibly because the case she was working on was so intense.

He took her into his arms, not saying a word. And she wrapped her arms around him, leaning on his strength.

"I'm glad you made it," he said.

"Of course. This is the only place I want to be tonight." She looked up at him and smiled. "Are the kids taken care of?"

"I believe Alethea is reading them a bedtime story. But she is not a nanny, Elle. She made sure to tell me that as she went to perform the task. This was after hovering around them at dinner trying to get them to eat their vegetables."

Elle laughed. "Of course."

"And tomorrow David and my mother will be by to take the children for the weekend. They wish to contribute to our alone time."

"Very nice of them."

"Indeed." He brushed his thumb over her cheek. "Are you ready to go out tonight?" He examined the faint shadows under her eyes. "Or would you rather stay in?"

"I would love to go out. Because I want to go show off my wonderful husband."

"You cannot possibly wish to do that more than I want to show off my wonderful wife."

"We'll have to argue about it later." She let out a sigh, a long, contented sound. "We've been together for more than ten years. It's amazing how different this last decade has been from the one before it."

"The one where we both wanted each other, but wouldn't allow ourselves to have each other?"

"Yes. I have no clue what we were so afraid of. What we were waiting for."

"The more I think about it, the more I believe we were waiting for the right time. Where we could be brave enough, give enough, love each other in the right way. Had I kissed you for the first time when I was twenty years old, I would have only messed it up later. I would not have been a man who could have given you the support you needed through all of this."

She nodded slowly. "I don't think I would have been a woman who could have gone for her dreams."

"Do you want to know a secret, Elle?"

She nodded. "Of course."

"I like everything that we have. I treasure it. I enjoy my job. I am proud of yours. But you're my dream."

Elle smiled, all of her exhaustion fading, tears filling her eyes. "Oh, Apollo. You're my dream, too."

She drew up on her toes and kissed him, and it was like the first time. Every time with her was like the first time.

"Perhaps we won't make it out after all," he said.

She smiled, her expression a little bit wicked. "Yes, perhaps it would be best if we stayed in."

* * * * *

MILLS & BOON®
Hardback – June 2016

ROMANCE

Bought for the Greek's Revenge	Lynne Graham
An Heir to Make a Marriage	Abby Green
The Greek's Nine-Month Redemption	Maisey Yates
Expecting a Royal Scandal	Caitlin Crews
Return of the Untamed Billionaire	Carol Marinelli
Signed Over to Santino	Maya Blake
Wedded, Bedded, Betrayed	Michelle Smart
The Surprise Conti Child	Tara Pammi
The Greek's Nine-Month Surprise	Jennifer Faye
A Baby to Save Their Marriage	Scarlet Wilson
Stranded with Her Rescuer	Nikki Logan
Expecting the Fellani Heir	Lucy Gordon
The Prince and the Midwife	Robin Gianna
His Pregnant Sleeping Beauty	Lynne Marshall
One Night, Twin Consequences	Annie O'Neil
Twin Surprise for the Single Doc	Susanne Hampton
The Doctor's Forbidden Fling	Karin Baine
The Army Doc's Secret Wife	Charlotte Hawkes
A Pregnancy Scandal	Kat Cantrell
A Bride for the Boss	Maureen Child

0516 GEN STD HB

MILLS & BOON®
Large Print – June 2016

ROMANCE

Leonetti's Housekeeper Bride	Lynne Graham
The Surprise De Angelis Baby	Cathy Williams
Castelli's Virgin Widow	Caitlin Crews
The Consequence He Must Claim	Dani Collins
Helios Crowns His Mistress	Michelle Smart
Illicit Night with the Greek	Susanna Carr
The Sheikh's Pregnant Prisoner	Tara Pammi
Saved by the CEO	Barbara Wallace
Pregnant with a Royal Baby!	Susan Meier
A Deal to Mend Their Marriage	Michelle Douglas
Swept into the Rich Man's World	Katrina Cudmore

HISTORICAL

Marriage Made in Rebellion	Sophia James
A Too Convenient Marriage	Georgie Lee
Redemption of the Rake	Elizabeth Beacon
Saving Marina	Lauri Robinson
The Notorious Countess	Liz Tyner

MEDICAL

Playboy Doc's Mistletoe Kiss	Tina Beckett
Her Doctor's Christmas Proposal	Louisa George
From Christmas to Forever?	Marion Lennox
A Mummy to Make Christmas	Susanne Hampton
Miracle Under the Mistletoe	Jennifer Taylor
His Christmas Bride-to-Be	Abigail Gordon

MILLS & BOON®
Hardback – July 2016

ROMANCE

0616 GEN STD HB

MILLS & BOON®
Large Print – July 2016

ROMANCE

The Italian's Ruthless Seduction	Miranda Lee
Awakened by Her Desert Captor	Abby Green
A Forbidden Temptation	Anne Mather
A Vow to Secure His Legacy	Annie West
Carrying the King's Pride	Jennifer Hayward
Bound to the Tuscan Billionaire	Susan Stephens
Required to Wear the Tycoon's Ring	Maggie Cox
The Greek's Ready-Made Wife	Jennifer Faye
Crown Prince's Chosen Bride	Kandy Shepherd
Billionaire, Boss...Bridegroom?	Kate Hardy
Married for Their Miracle Baby	Soraya Lane

HISTORICAL

The Secrets of Wiscombe Chase	Christine Merrill
Rake Most Likely to Sin	Bronwyn Scott
An Earl in Want of a Wife	Laura Martin
The Highlander's Runaway Bride	Terri Brisbin
Lord Crayle's Secret World	Lara Temple

MEDICAL

A Daddy for Baby Zoe?	Fiona Lowe
A Love Against All Odds	Emily Forbes
Her Playboy's Proposal	Kate Hardy
One Night...with Her Boss	Annie O'Neil
A Mother for His Adopted Son	Lynne Marshall
A Kiss to Change Her Life	Karin Baine

MILLS & BOON®

Why shop at millsandboon.co.uk?

Each year, thousands of romance readers find their perfect read at millsandboon.co.uk. That's because we're passionate about bringing you the very best romantic fiction. Here are some of the advantages of shopping at www.millsandboon.co.uk:

* **Get new books first**—you'll be able to buy your favourite books one month before they hit the shops

* **Get exclusive discounts**—you'll also be able to buy our specially created monthly collections, with up to 50% off the RRP

* **Find your favourite authors**—latest news, interviews and new releases for all your favourite authors and series on our website, plus ideas for what to try next

* **Join in**—once you've bought your favourite books, don't forget to register with us to rate, review and join in the discussions

Visit **www.millsandboon.co.uk**
for all this and more today!